TAKEN HOME BY THE GRIZZLY

OBSESSED MOUNTAIN MATES

ARIANA HAWKES

Imprint: Independently published

ISBN: 9798879098372

Cover art: Thunderface Design

www.arianahawkes.com

Zoe

I swear it's cold enough to freeze the nards off an elk this morning. I'm huddled in my ugly-but-warm parka and knitted hat, but I'm still shivering as I shuffle along the sidewalk, trying my best not to faceplant in the snow.

The café I'm heading to is just across the little town square, but it might as well be on the other side of the Arctic. In between is a dazzling, sparkling display of festive lights and decorations. Real pretty, except that every little thing I see taunts me, reminding me, *Christmas is over, and you don't live here anymore, Zoe.*

I pass the huge Christmas tree in the center, trying not to look at its gorgeous glittery splendor, and I'm less than fifty yards from the café when…

Thunk! something hits me right in the face.

"What the—?" White powder explodes in front of my eyes. *A snowball?* My cheek stings like crazy. Feels like there was plenty of ice packed into it.

I clutch my face and look around wildly, trying to identify the thrower of the missile.

"Ha-hah!" comes a loud voice off to my left. A child stands, right arm raised, poised to lob another snow rocket at me. I say child. He's almost my height.

"You little...!" I holler. I crouch down, snatch up a handful of snow and pack it into a hard sphere. Then I straighten up and prepare to launch.

He gives a shriek of fear.

Oh God, he's actually pretty young. He's probably only ten or something. *What am I doing?* I drop the snowball in horror. *Always on the defensive, Zoe. Always ready to act first, think later.*

A lady rushes over. She's wearing an expensive-looking coat and tall leather boots. "Oh, there you are Lucas!" she exclaims.

To my dismay, the little brat starts whimpering.

"What's the matter, honey?"

He jabs a quivering finger at me. "That mean lady was about to hurt me."

"What?" I squeak in outrage. "He started it!"

She looks me up and down with disdain. "You should know better at your age."

I open my mouth to point out that her little angel almost blinded me with a mini iceberg.

What's the point, though? Some people only see what they want to see.

Instead, I hunch my shoulders and leave them to their charade.

When I pull open the door of the café, a waft of warm air and the smell of freshly baked cookies greets me. I love this dang place. It's buzzing, but right away, I locate my best friend, Chrissie. That's because she's sitting in our usual corner. She looks up at the same moment and we give each other a sad little wave. When I arrive at the table, I see that Chrissie has already ordered a coffee for me. And donuts. It's so sweet, my eyes sting. I blink fast before I start crying like an idiot.

"Why is your cheek all red?" she asks as I sit down.

"Oh, it's nothing." I wave my hand. "I've got bigger fish to fry." Like the fact we both got laid off from our jobs yesterday.

"Been doing some thinking?" she asks.

"Yup. I'm thinking there's no way I'm going to get another job right after the holidays. You?"

"Yeah, same." She laces her fingers together and stares into the middle distance. "Soo... I've been talking to Jack. His family always rents out a cabin in Vermont in January, and they do a ton of skiing. He's invited me to go stay with them for the month."

"That's... that's great, Chrissie," I say, my chest warming. "I'm really happy for you." She and Jack haven't had an easy ride. He's been the definition of emotionally unavailable so far. But sounds like things are finally coming together for them.

Chrissie reaches out and lays her hand on mine. "And I want you to come, too, Zoe. There'll be tons of space, and Jack says they're good people—"

"No." I cut her off. "That's so, so kind of you, but no way am I gatecrashing your first visit with your boyfriend's family."

Her eyes turn huge and liquid. "But, Zoe, I don't want to leave you alone. We had plans together."

"We were just gonna roast a chicken and watch some Christmas movies or something." We worked the entire holiday season, so we were planning to have a late Christmas in January, just the two of us.

She rolls her eyes. "Doesn't matter. We promised to spend it together."

"But sometimes life throws a spanner in the works." Like a gigantic, unemployment-shaped spanner. "Don't worry, I'll figure something out."

"Like what?"

I let out an elephantine sigh. "I mean, you're right, no one's hiring right after the holidays. I was up all night going through the job sites. But there's just nothing." Annnd my rent is due, and there's no way I'll be able to make it. But I don't want to tell her that.

"So...?" She lifts her shoulders and looks at me beseechingly.

"No," I say firmly. "And that's final."

Her eyes narrow. "I think there's something you're not telling me."

Darn. She knows me too well. "Actually, there was this one job..."

"What for?" she says eagerly.

"Oh, no. It's not right for me."

"Zoe, you're so talented, but you always sell yourself short. Here, let me have a look."

With a sigh, I pick up my phone, scroll to the job ad and hand it over to her.

"Nanny wanted for winter season. Competitive rates of pay and comfortable accommodation in traditional mountain home. All-expenses-paid. Must love lively children," she reads out loud.

I give a violent shudder.

"But this is perfect! Job and accommodation in one." Her eyes are sparkling with enthusiasm.

"Except that I have zero experience or ability to deal with kids."

Chrissie shrugs. "Kids are easy. You just have fun with them and make sure they don't kill themselves, or each other."

I groan. "You say that because you come from a big family. I was an only child."

"*Exactly!* You were a child once. Just remember what you liked. What made you happy."

I *was* a child, but that whole formative years thing ended early for me. That's the part I don't tell Chrissie about. Despite her best efforts to get it out of me, I never talk about my past. Ever since I reached adulthood, I've just wanted to focus on the future. Focus on getting through life without feeling like a total freak. And I always knew I never wanted to have kids.

"Maybe it will be good for you."

I sigh. "Who the hell is going to employ me?"

"Someone who sees what a good heart you have, and how dedicated you are to everything you do."

I snort, remembering how I almost pelted a small child in the face with a snowball as big as his head.

"Pity the kid who ends up with me," I mutter.

"Just give them a call, Zoe. At least find out if you get on with each other."

I finish up the last dregs of my coffee. "Think I'll just go around town today, see if anyone wants to hire me to do anything at all."

I follow Chrissie's gaze to the window. It's snowing *again*, and it looks like a freezing, gray wilderness out there.

"O…kay," she says.

* * *

TWENTY-FOUR HOURS LATER, I've ascertained that there is categorically no work available in this town. Not a big surprise. I already knew there was a ton of unemployment here. And that ad I've favorited on my phone is burning a hole in my pocket.

I close my eyes. Try to conjure up positive thoughts. A warm, cozy home, full of fun and laughter. A couple of sweet-natured kids. A fire crackling in the hearth. Festive decorations still up.

I pick up my phone and tap out the number. Can't hurt, right?

A woman answers, in a bored-sounding drawl. "Yeah, the job's still available."

"Great—"

"Can you start tomorrow?"

"T-tomorrow?" My head whirls. "Don't you want to see my resumé first?"

"Yeah, I guess," she says around a yawn.

"I'll email it now."

I wait on the line while she mutters her way through the eccentric list of jobs I've held down in my short life: dishwasher, dog shelter cleaner, bike courier, gift-shop assistant. "Yeah, sounds good," she says after a few seconds.

Sounds good? How can that sound good? I don't have an iota of relevant experience.

"How many children do you have?" I ask.

"Uh…" She pauses as if she's not sure, herself. "Three."

My stomach tightens. For someone who thinks one child will be a big responsibility, three is… is…inconceivable.

I swallow down a burst of panic. "Maybe we can video chat, so I can meet the little ones first?" I say in my brightest voice.

"Nah, won't be necessary."

"You want to think about it for a while?" I ask when she doesn't say anything else.

"No, the job's yours. Be here tomorrow at three p.m."

I blink. "That's kinda short notice. Can I start the day after?"

"No. You gotta be there then."

"I need some time to figure out logistics—" I start to say, but she's already ended the call.

Wow. I might not be the greatest nanny the world has ever known, but thank goodness I'm not a psychopath or an axe murderer. Maybe it's a good thing they're hiring me after all.

I cast around the tiny, one room studio that has been

my home for the past year. That was hands down the weirdest job interview of my life, and I feel like I'm in way over my head. But what choice do I have?

I grab my keys and head out to the local bookshop, where I'm hoping they have a childcare section.

2

Lock

*F*ive days ago, there was nothing here but peace, quiet and snow. Just me in my beary world. Holed up in my fortress. Hunting, sleeping, hating the world. Nothing new there. I like this time of year. I sleep a lot. Gives me a break from my fucked-up thoughts.

But something just dragged me out of my semi-hibernation:

Vehicles, driving through the middle of the damn forest. Fancy trucks, with off-road tires, tearing through the snow. I hauled myself up to the window and watched as they pulled up in front of the house opposite. Some human dude got out of the first truck and fitted a key into the padlocked gate. Took him a while to drag the rusty old chain off and haul the gates open, then they were through, heading up the driveway and parking in the yard.

What the hell are they doing here? No one's been up to this old house before. I thought it was abandoned. From the outside, it's a nice, fancy log cabin, but inside it's all run down, everything trashed and neglected. I know this because when I first arrived, I climbed over the fence and peered through all the windows. I make it my business to know what's going on in my territory. There were no signs that anyone had been living there for a long, long time. And as the months passed, and no one arrived to claim it, I started to relax. To forget it was even there.

But now, a woman is climbing out of the other truck and stretching. She's a small human, also wearing fancy city clothes. And… what's that? She opens the rear door and three rugrats spill out. Even worse.

Immediately, they start running around, chasing each other and screaming their little heads off. This is a lot more than I can stand right now.

When they all go toward the house, I lose sight of them. I shove open the front door of my cabin and step outside for the first time in three days. My muscles ache from underuse as I hurry along the boundary fence of their property, seeking out a better vantage point. There, I see the human man—a weedy-looking guy, as most humans are—opening up the front door.

The female wrinkles her nose. "Smells musty," she says.

"Well, no one's been in here for a long time," the guy

replies. "But we'll start up the furnace, make a fire in the den."

"We should've gotten someone to deal with this before we arrived!" she snaps.

"Well, we're here now. We'll settle in soon." The man calls the rugrats to him and they step inside the house, shutting the front door behind them.

I stand there watching, wondering what the hell they're up to. Surely they're not planning to stay in this rundown place? Can't imagine any humans staying there, let alone people who look like they're used to a whole lot of comfort and fancy things. Maybe they're just checking it out? Maybe one of them inherited it, and they're planning to sell it? I wait a while, expecting them to leave at some point. But after a couple of hours, they haven't come out.

And, as dusk falls, the lights in the house click on. They're going to stay here overnight.

I swear every follicle of my beast's shaggy fur stands on end.

You know how long it's been since another two-legged being slept within a hundred yards of me? No, I don't either. I've gotten used to being the only human-slash-shifter around here, and that's the way I like it.

All night long, I toss and turn on my mattress, feeling like I'm lying on a nest of goddamn fire ants. Wondering what they want with the house next door. Wondering if there's anything I can do to get rid of them. My instincts are telling me to get the hell out of this place. To seek out somewhere more secluded. Build another cabin with my bare hands, far, far away from any kind of civilization.

The next morning, I hear the sound of a vehicle pulling out of the yard. But it's only one of the trucks. And it's back an hour later. The man and woman unload a bunch of stuff from the truck and carry it into the house. Then, later that afternoon they bring out a stepladder and a bunch of wires and start fussing around the big ol' fir tree that sits in the yard. Soon, it's all lit up with colored lights. And I figure it out—must be that time of year. Holidays. The season when humans eat like there's a famine coming, and decorate their homes with brightly-colored crap.

The thought barrels at me: they're not leaving. They're settling in, and they're going to be here for the duration. I can't stand it, can't stand being so close to them. I pace up and down my cabin, snarling and fretting. Trying to gather my thoughts. But my head aches like hell.

Yup, I'm the archetypal bear with a sore head. I'm not supposed to be awake at this time of year. Not all shifters hibernate, but I figure I'm more than half beast. More like seventy-five percent. Most of the time I feel like I'm hanging on to my human side by a thread. Unfortunately, there's no one left in my family to ask about my DNA.

I need to go find a cave or something—somewhere where I can stay while I gather enough wood to build a new cabin. But I don't want to leave. I like it here. It took me months of searching to find it. I was hoping I'd find some kind of rough shelter, but there it was—a perfect little wood cabin, deep in the forest, with no sign that humans had been there for years. The only negative was the big house next door. But that also seemed abandoned—

What's that?

Something appears at my window. A human face. I dart behind the couch. I can't let them see me. If they know there's a bear in here, they'll probably hire someone to come take me out with a rifle.

Just like what happened before.

I hunker down and watch a snot-nosed little kid peering through my goddamn window. Cupping his hands around his eyes, his breath misting the glass. He'll go back and tell his parents there's a cabin here. Will they give a shit?

Of course, they will. Humans always want to stick their noses where they don't belong. Live and let live is not a human philosophy.

But if they see me as a man? Well, that's different. I've got as much right to be here as any other man.

Keeping my body low to the ground, I push my beast deep down inside me and let my human come out. It's a hell of a tussle. My bear doesn't like going back inside. And my human hasn't been out for months. Bones crunch, tendons snap, and I bite back a bellow. But at last, there I am, crouching down on all fours, flexing my muscles, checking everything's still in working order.

The little boy has moved on to another window. He's rubbing at the grime on the glass, like he owns the damn place. I stride to the door and yank it open. "What the hell do you think you're doing?" I holler.

"Whoa!" he exclaims, eyes just about bulging out of his head.

"I said, what are you doing trespassing on my property?" My voice comes out as my beast's roar. He looks terrified, but I don't give a crap. I need to make sure this never happens again.

"Answer me!"

"I-I didn't mean to," he stutters, and runs.

I stand on my porch, watching as he hightails it all the way to the big house. Good. Hope that's the last I'll see of him.

I pace around my cabin. I'm all riled up. My beast is busting to go run, clawing at me from the inside. But I can't take the risk right now, in case those humans see me.

At some point, I must've fallen asleep. Happens a lot during the winter months. It's an uneasy sleep, full of nightmares from the past. I toss and turn, and twitch on my mattress. Something's coming after my clan with a gigantic hammer. Beating, beating at the ground. My eyes fly open. No, not a hammer. Someone is knocking at the door.

It's pitch dark outside now. I grab my rifle. After everything that happened to my family, I can't be too careful. I flip on the porch light and yank open the door. There he is—human man, standing right on my doorstep. Stupid fake smile plastered to his face.

But at the sight of me, his smile drops and his mouth falls open. Guess I'm a sight for sore eyes in my human form. Haven't had my hair cut or trimmed my beard since who knows when.

"What do you want?" I growl.

"Uh, I'm sorry, I didn't—" He turns, like he's about to leave.

I take a step closer. There's no way he's leaving until I find out the truth. "Now you're on my property, you're gonna tell me what you're doing here."

"Oh, my little boy, Todd, said we had a neighbor. I thought I'd come introduce myself. But I can see we're bothering you. But..." He keeps looking me up and down.

Yeah, I'm holding a gun, and I'm naked, as always. But what did he expect? My grandaddy's last words are inked on the nape of my neck—*Shouldn't have taken claws to a gunfight*—and it's not a credo I'm gonna forget in a hurry.

"Is there a problem?" I growl.

The dude puts his hand to his throat, like he's choking. "I don't think it's, uh, appropriate that you're naked and all, in front of my son."

A roar bursts from my lips, and he jumps. "Your son was staring through my window like a peeping Tom. Maybe you should ask him about that."

He blinks behind his expensive-looking glasses. "He's just a little kid."

"Who needs better parenting!" I bellow. "This is my property. I was living here in peace, until you folks turned up. If I want to be goddamn naked, I will be. If you know what's good for you, you'll teach your kids not to trespass."

The man has turned real pale. He doesn't say

anything else; he just turns and scurries away. Like a scared little rabbit.

That's the last I'll see of them, I tell myself. And the thought rises up in me, clear and strong:

No way am I leaving this place.

No way am I getting chased out of here by a bunch of self-righteous humans. I'm going to stand my ground, do right by my family. I'm the only one left from my clan. And I'm not gonna be the one to run.

3

Zoe

ichelle, my brand-new boss, is hurtling around the house like a tornado. There's an expensive-looking duffle bag slung over her shoulder, and she's shouting instructions to her hubby as she goes. Kinda get the impression she's eager to get out of here.

"What about bedtimes?" I call. I'm sitting on the edge of the couch, smiling at the three kids encouragingly. Not that they notice. They're running around the house like they just necked super-size sodas.

"Huh?" She stops and scowls at me.

"I said, what time to they each go to bed?"

"Oh…" She flaps a hand, irritated. "Whenever they're tired."

Okay. Another non-specific answer to add to my list. So far, she doesn't have any rules on screen time, bath-times, or bedtimes. She doesn't mind what they eat, and they don't have any allergies that she's aware of, *but who knows with kids?*

"When will you be back?" I ask.

"In a coupla weeks…"

I goggle at her. "Wha—?"

She turns her head to the stairs. "Adrian!" she bawls.

I finger the envelope she's just given me. It's stuffed with a wad of cash. Two-thousand bucks, she told me. That's double what I was expecting.

Her hubby hurries down the stairs, carrying two suitcases. He flicks me a sheepish glance.

"Anything else at all that I need to know about the kids?" I'm begging now.

She plasters a huge smile on her face. "You'll figure it out."

"You see a rundown cabin on your way up here?" Adrian fixes me with a serious look.

"Yeah," I say slowly. I do remember passing a cabin as I trudged up the hill to the property, lugging my duffel bag. I'd been walking a *long* way from the Greyhound bus stop, and I was almost delirious with cold and tiredness, but it caught my attention. The windows were dim, but I swear I saw a face behind the glass, watching me. It should've been creepy, but it felt cozy, somehow. Homely.

"If you know what's good for you, stay away from it," he mutters.

"Why?" I ask.

"Just stay away from it," he says cryptically.

Okay. Well, that's the least of my worries right now.

He hauls open the front door, and they're gone.

"I didn't agree to this," I tell no one at all. I stand in the open doorway, watching dazedly as my new employers climb into one of their trucks and pull away.

They didn't even say goodbye to their kids.

The last hour has been one of the strangest episodes of my life, and that's saying a lot, considering my upbringing made Alice's journey through Wonderland look like a guided tour with a map.

Funny, when I arrived here, and saw the lit-up fir tree in the yard, my chest warmed. I thought, this is a good family. A family that cares about making things nice. How wrong I was.

The minute the parents are out of sight, the kids stream past me and bound into the yard like overexcited puppies. One of them clambers on top of his mom's truck, while the other starts scaling the fir tree. The first one is Jace, while his twin brother is Todd. They're wearing different clothes, luckily. As for their older sister, Mari, she's heading toward the far corner, where the woodpile is.

"Jace, come down from there, you might put a dent in the roof," I call.

He flashes me a look, then jumps up and down on the roof with both feet.

Oh, god.

I rush over and step up on the running board, trying to reach for him. Of course, he ducks away from me.

"Haha! can't catch me!"

Behind me, I hear a rustling sound and spin around in time to see Todd scrambling up to the highest branches of the fir tree. They don't look strong enough to support him.

"Todd, come down from there, please," I call.

"You're not my mom!" he shrieks.

"You can't tell us what to do," Jace yells from behind me.

I close my eyes for a beat, disengage myself from the situation, just like the childcare book advised. "No, I'm not your mom, but I'm taking care of you in place of your mom. Which means that it's my job to keep you safe. And because I'm an adult, I'm better at this kind of stuff than you guys. Please come down here, and we can go play a game together."

Both of them completely blank me and carry on with what they were doing. *Crap.* What now?

What now is that I discover the parents left the front gates open when they exited, and Mari is no longer playing on the woodpile. In fact, I can see a set of tiny footprints exiting the gate and heading down the hill. *No!* Panic screams through my brain.

"You two, get down from there right now!" I yell. The childcare book would definitely not condone this, but desperate times and all that...

To my huge relief, Jace clambers down from the truck and Todd leaps down from the tree. I swear it's at least an eight-foot drop, but he lands like it's nothing and takes off toward the gate.

"Stay close," I tell the two of them, and I start to

follow after Mari's tiny footprints, which bear right into the forest.

The twins race on ahead of me, and I try to keep an eye on them while following the footprints. I'm so intent on my task that I don't see the mysterious log cabin until it's right in front of me.

It's rustic. But actually not *rundown* like my new boss said. There are curtains up at the little square windows, and the window panes aren't cracked or broken.

"That's where the scary man lives," Todd exclaims.

My breath catches. "What scary man?"

"A wild man. He's all hairy and he doesn't wear clothes."

Oh, my God. And Mari's steps go directly to the porch. Is she in there? I stare at the front door, horror gathering in my insides. Did this crazy naked wild man snatch her?

What if he's got her? What if he's hurting her right now?

My heart beats fast. I fumble for my phone. I need to call the police.

With trembling fingers, I dial 911.

The call doesn't connect. Fuck. The signal here is virtually non-existent. I try again and again, but it's the same useless *beep-beep-beep.*

"Kids, I want you to run back into the house and shut the door. And do not answer it until you hear my voice shouting you, okay?"

Two pairs of huge brown eyes stare back at me. *Good.* They've dropped their insolent act and they know I'm serious. "Go on."

They don't need telling twice, they turn and sprint back the way they came.

I take a deep breath and rap on the door. My heart is hammering like a jackhammer and I wonder if I'm experiencing my last few minutes on earth.

The door swings open on creaking hinges, and I jump. It wasn't locked.

"Hello?" I call. There's only silence within. There's a light showing through a doorway at the back though. Crap.

I step inside and the door bangs shut behind me.

My legs are trembling. But I've gotta do this, gotta make sure Mari is not here.

It's a bare kind of place. Not a whole lot of furniture. Some force stronger than my sense of self-preservation propels me through the cabin, and toward the doorway at the rear.

Holding my breath, I push the door open.

It's a bedroom. Not much more than a bed in there, but it's got a comforter on top, and it smells clean. No closets, or cupboards. I crouch down and look under the bed. No small child tied up there. Through another doorway is a bathroom. Also small and basic but clean.

She's not here.

Relief pours through me. But where the hell is she?

I need to keep looking outside. I sprint through the cabin, out the front door and… almost collide with the huge, half-naked wild man standing right in my path. I skid to a stop.

In his arms is a shivering Mari. She's soaking wet, drenched, from head to toe.

"She's safe," the man says. Only, his voice is more of a growl than human speech. Like an avalanche of boulders tumbling down a hill.

"What happened? Are you okay, honey?" I gasp out.

"You need to take better care of your kids, lady."

"I-I was taking care of them," I stutter. Right now, I don't have the words to explain that I was trying to take care of them, while all three of them were doing their best to take themselves out. "They're very lively kids," I say instead. "What happened?"

"She went for a dip in the river, that's what," he grunts, looking at me like I'm the worst carer in the world.

"I wanted to swim!" Mari says in her shrill voice.

"You weren't even supposed to be outside the gate, never mind swimming," I say. "But come on, let's get you dried off and warmed up."

I go to take her from the scary mountain man, but he holds her away from me.

"Don't know if you're fit to be looking after her," he grunts.

I open my mouth to tell him it's none of his business. Then I stop. Recalibrate.

"Look, I'm the new nanny. I just got here—"

"And the parents just left," he butts in.

"Yeah, they've gone on vacation or something."

"You weren't expecting that, huh?"

I blink. He's sure perceptive for a crazy mountain man. "No, I wasn't. And it's gonna take me a while to get used to these kids and their routines," I say. "But I promise you, I'm gonna do the darn best job I can. So can you please give Mari to me?"

His eyes—his weirdly gorgeous eyes—narrow as they lock onto mine in a cool, assessing stare. He looks, and looks, and gooseflesh breaks out on my skin. I've never felt so scrutinized in my life. I think I even stop breathing.

Then something flickers in his expression. Something softer. Is it sympathy? His irises glow with an intense green-gold hue, and it makes no sense at all, but I feel like he's seeing me. Seeing past all my issues and neuroses and hurt, and glimpsing the heart of who I really am.

He gives a deep nod and hands her over. "Sorry if I judged you prematurely and all."

My heart flutters. "It's okay. Guess I can see where you're coming from." I take a breath, realizing, amid all of this craziness, that he actually saved Mari's life. "And thank you *so much* for saving her."

"You're welcome. Good thing I heard the splash."

Mari is trembling like crazy, her teeth chattering.

"I'd better get her indoors," I tell him, and I turn and run back to the house, as fast as I can go with a sixty-pound weight in my arms.

"You can't go doing things like that, Mari. You'll get yourself into a lot of danger," I scold.

She looks up at me earnestly. "I like him. Can we go stay with him?"

"What? No! He's a mountain man. He likes being all alone and stuff. And your parents have hired me to look after you."

"I think you should marry him."

"W-why do you say that?"

"He likes you. He thinks you're pretty."

My heart gives a weird little jump. "That's not true," I mumble. Then I remember the look he was giving me —beneath all that hostility and confusion.

Intense, unwavering. Like he could hardly tear his eyes away from me. Running over my features like he wanted to memorize them. Even as I turned away, I felt his burning gaze on my body. I'm not pretty. I'm average, kinda dumpy. But for the first time in my life, I felt like a queen.

And, gosh, he's good looking, too. Those green eyes blazing below straight, dark brows. A flash of nice, white teeth behind his dark beard. Messy, dark hair. Man, I wouldn't mind finger-combing the tangles out of that. And what a body. After he handed Mari to me, his bare torso was exposed in all its muscly glory. Huge pecs and biceps. Rippling abs.

Far hotter than any crazy mountain man has the right to be.

I'm at the gate now, puffing out white clouds of breath like a steam engine. My legs are about ready to give way as I stumble across the yard in a half-run, Mari wrapped around me like a marmoset.

At last, I'm through the door.

"Todd, Jace, you here?" I call.

"Yeah!" Two little voices echo down from the second story. Thank goodness. I shut the door, lock it and close up the bolt at the top. I dread to think what they've been up to since I've been gone, but I can't think about that right now. Instead, I hurry to the bathroom.

I plant Mari down on the toilet lid and I put the plug in the bathtub and turn the faucet.

And a load of brown pours out.

Great. Guess it hasn't been used in a while.

Eventually, it turns clear, but it's ice cold. In fact, the whole freaking house is cold. Is there a furnace, or something?

"I'm cold," Mari whines.

Resisting the urge to ask what she expected from jumping in a river fully clothed, I pull a clean towel off the airer and help her to strip off her wet clothes. Then I wrap the towel around her and rub her down, until I'm satisfied that she's dry. "Better?" I ask.

She nods. I get her to show me where her room is and we find some dry clothes. Not ideal, but it's all I've got until I figure out how to get the hot water to work.

THE NEXT HALF hour could be a supplementary episode to Dante's Inferno. Watching three extremely energetic and undisciplined kids, while trying to figure out how the hell to get the furnace started pushes me to the brink of my sanity. I *think* I'm doing the right thing, but the furnace just won't light.

I call the parents again, and again. But either they don't have connection in their truck, or they've switched their phones off. And it's dark outside now and getting colder. Crap.

I google furnace technicians. It takes a while because each page takes thirty seconds to open, but I ascertain that there's absolutely no one able or willing to come out here, until after the weekend.

Trying to ignore the little voice telling me just how dumb I was to have accepted this job, I race up to the kitchen and fill the kettle. Then I hunt around for pans. Maybe I can boil enough hot water to fill the bathtub.

Trouble is, there are no big pans, only two small saucepans.

"I'm hungry," Todd whines from behind me.

"There any cookies you can eat?" I mutter, rooting in a cupboard.

"I dunno." There's a scrabbling sound, followed by a loud crash. I flip around. Todd is on top of the counter, and a glass bottle is lying shattered on the ground, spilling a syrupy pool of liquid across the floor.

"So-rree," Todd says, looking not at all sorry.

"No climbing on the counter," I say, more snappily than I intended.

His face crumples and he lets out an ear-splitting wail.

Holy crap.

I stare at him in dismay. He's turning purple with outrage, but there are no tears there. He's just spoiled. Not used to being told no.

"Stay right there," I tell him, as I go look for a dustpan and broom.

The wailing cuts out immediately. "You said no climbing on the counter," he says in a mocking voice.

"It's okay. For the next five minutes, it's okay." I'm struggling to keep my voice level.

Riiinng!

My head jerks around. "What's that?"

Todd rolls his eyes and raises his hands like a sassy teen. "Doorbell?"

I frown. Where did he learn that?

Riiiinng! it goes again. What now? My head feels like it's going to explode.

I take off for the front door at a run.

I yank back the bolt, turn the latch, and... my eyes just about fall out of my head.

Because it's *him*.

The crazy mountain man.

Only now, he doesn't look quite so crazy. He's no longer half-naked. Instead, he's wearing a blue button-down and black pants. His hair looks combed, and if I'm not mistaken, he's trimmed his beard, so I can see his lips, which are full, and distractingly *sexy*—

I give myself a shake. Can't go thinking about stuff like that now. Need to focus on what he's doing, standing on the doorstep, one elbow propped against the doorframe.

Darn, he looks good doing that, all casual.

Then his gaze locks onto mine.

He stares at me like I'm the only thing that exists in the whole world. Like he's in love with me or something. I literally see his pupils dilate, turning his irises dark.

My mouth goes all dry.

He wants me.

I'm not the kind of girl that guys go crazy over, but this sexy mountain man looks like he's dying to tear my clothes off and ravish me. The thought pours through me like liquid fire.

Before I know it, I'm imagining him hauling me off to his cabin and doing all kinds of naughty things to me—

"Sorry to bother you," he says. "Thought you might need some help."

I snap back to the present. To the unruly kids and the freezing cold house. "Where did you get that idea?" I hear the rising hysteria in my own voice.

He raises his hands and lets them fall to his thighs. "I know this place is kinda run down. Some things might need fixing."

My head spins.

I want to grab him by his sexy bicep and haul him inside.

But he's a stranger. Yes, a stranger who rescued Mari. But that doesn't mean I should let him in the house. My first duty is to protect these children.

"No, I'm fine," I tell him. "I'm figuring things out. We'll be okay."

He narrows his eyes and fixes me with that intense look of his. The one that has a magical ability to turn my knees to Jell-O. "Sure? Don't need help with the furnace? Getting the fire going?

My breath hitches. *He's talking about the heating system, not your own personal furnace—which is going pretty well right now.*

Yes! I want to scream.

All of the above. And maybe you could keep an eye on at least one of these children. Because keeping all three of them out of mischief seems to be a mission impossible.

"No, I've got it all in hand," I force my mouth to say.

"Really?" For a fleeting moment, he tears his gaze away from me and peers into the darkness of the house.

"Yup, really."

"Okay." His face fills with what looks like disappointment. But who on earth feels disappointed at not having to fix a furnace? "I'm Lock, by the way. Let me know if you change your mind."

"I will," I say automatically.

He raises an eyebrow, a slight quirk to his lips. "Is it a secret?"

"Huh?"

"Your name."

"Oh." My cheeks flare in the cold like a beacon. "It's Zoe."

A light comes into his eyes. "Real pretty name."

"T-thanks," I stutter. Gosh, that stare. It's killing my brain cells.

"Well, have a good night, Zoe." He gives me one more long look, his gaze tracing the length of my body and back again. Then he turns and leaves.

For some reason I stand there, watching him disappear into the dark night, my heart plummeting to my boots.

"Goodbye, hot mountain man," I whisper.

He stops and turns.

And waves.

Oh, my god. He heard me.

Crap, crap, crap.

My cheeks flame even hotter as I slam the door shut.

4

Lock

*Z*oe. Zoe. Zoe.

A beautiful name for a beautiful girl. I say it over and over, reveling in the sound. My bear can growl it out—which it does, repeatedly. But I don't tell it to quit. I could listen to her name all day long.

Zoe, my girl. My mate.

I'm sitting on my porch with a beer, looking up at the icy sky and replaying every precious moment I just spent with her.

I picture her as clearly as if I was looking at a photo. Those huge blue eyes, full of intelligence and humor. The freckles scattered across her cute little nose. Those full pink lips. And that, sexy, sexy body of hers. Tight and curvy in all the right places.

I can hardly believe it, but she's mine.

The one I'm supposed to be with.

She's not a beast like me, but the most perfect, incredible thing I've ever seen.

Young and still untouched, but so ripe to be mated. Her peach blossom scent is driving my animal insane. Now it's chosen its mate, it's unstoppable. It won't quit urging me to go break her door down and throw her over my shoulder. Claim her sweet cherry and impregnate her at the same time.

I imagine her pregnant. That tiny little belly of hers swelling with my young. She's so good with these kids, I can tell she'll be a great mother. Perfect little angel on the outside; fierce mama bear on the inside.

Hold yer horses, Lock.

You gotta kiss her first.

I close my eyes, imagining it all. Those rosebud lips parting under my own feral ones. Her body pressing up against mine.

God knows I don't deserve a princess like her.

But maybe she likes rugged guys.

Hot mountain man, she called me, when she thought I couldn't hear. Guess she's right. Well, the mountain man part anyway. Tried to clean myself up a little before I went to see her though. Showered, brushed my teeth, trimmed my beard.

I was trying to look civilized. Then I almost screwed it up, because I couldn't stop staring at her. At those pretty eyes, flashing with stress and frustration. At the sarcastic quirk in her lips. She's struggling, but not letting it get to her. She hasn't lost her sense of humor.

I want to take all that stress away from her. Let her know she's not alone. That I'm here to protect her.

I went around the house, checking if there was an external entrance to the basement, so I could go in and fix the furnace without bothering her. But no. She'll have to let me in.

When she trusts me.

They'll be okay tonight. The kids aren't gonna freeze. Even the little scamp who fell in the river.

But I want them to be warm and comfortable. Especially her. I want to wrap her up in my comforter. Press her up against my big grizzly chest.

Imagine that. Her naked between my sheets.

I've never had a woman before. Never thought it could be a part of my life.

Now all I can think about is burying my cock in her and making her mine.

I gaze at the stars, looking deeper and deeper into the galaxies.

Can I really allow myself to believe it's true—that fate is smiling down on me at last?

Life has often seemed like one hard knock after another. I thought my whole family line was cursed. But is it possible this perfect little human could be my mate—?

I go still.

What's that sound? One rusted piece of metal grinding against another one.

A key, turning in a padlock. Then a muttered, "come on."

Zoe's voice. It enters my ears like the sweetest music.

I stop breathing, and my beast quits its relentless pacing, and I savor every little sound. Her sighs of frustration. A click as the lock slides open. A muttered *thank goodness.*

Maybe she's gonna drive somewhere. I tamp down on my eagerness, waiting, waiting.

Then I hear her footsteps in the snow, going slow. Downhill.

My beast surges inside me.

She's coming.

I DASH INDOORS, put my beer away. Brush my teeth fast —make sure my breath smells nice and fresh for her. Then I sit back down on the porch, and wait. My beast is desperate to run to her, of course. Lead her safely through the dark, snowy path. But I've got to rein in my animal impulses. It's real important that I don't scare her just now. I need her to trust me. To understand that I would never hurt a single hair on her head.

I hear her footsteps, *crunch, crunch, crunching* through the virgin snow. Then I spot a little beam of light chasing through the forest. She must have brought a torch with her. Smart girl. I hold still, every nerve in my body aching for her. I've never wanted to see anything as much as I want to see her right now.

Here she is. Treading cautiously in her winter boots, wrapped up in a coat that looks like a big brown comforter.

Go to her, my beast insists. *Snatch her up and carry her into the cabin.*

I silence it with a snarl. *That's not how you treat a human female.* However much I might want to. However much my cock is straining against my zipper, dying to get between her thighs.

Instead, I let her come to me.

At last, she arrives at the porch, uncertainty showing in those beautiful blue eyes. "I need your help," she says.

The heavens ring above my head. "Anything. Just say the word."

I see her chest rise and fall as she takes a big breath. "You're right, I can't get the furnace to work. It's freezing cold in the house, and there's no hot water. I was wondering if you had any ideas?"

"I'm pretty good with my hands," I say casually.

I see her gaze dart to them, and I wonder what she's thinking. Is she wondering how they'll feel running all over her?

Then she bites her lip. And I see it. The tell-tale flush of desire creeping up her cheeks. That's *exactly* what she's thinking.

She wants me.

Then the scent of her need hits my nostrils.

Holy crap.

My loins burn and my vision goes dark.

My beast's thick hide burns my skin. *She's yours. Claim her.*

Lust is consuming me. The whole world contracts to a point, this need to drag her inside and possess her.

But first, she needs my help.

With a massive effort, I rein everything back.

"Lead the way," I say.

"Thank you, that's real kind of you." she says quietly, then her gaze flickers to the front door, which is wide open. "You got a fire going in there?"

"Sure have." It's actually the first fire I've lit all winter. When I'm in my bear form, I don't feel the cold one bit. But as a human, I appreciate its warm glow.

"Looks cozy," she says, wistfully.

"If you didn't have those cubs to look after, I'd invite you in." *And strip you naked in front of the fire.*

"Cubs?"

"I mean kids," I say quickly.

"Speaking of which, I need to get back. I hate the fact that I've left them alone, but there was no way I was going to drag them out in the cold."

"They'll be okay," I tell her. "You're doing a real good job."

She gives a dry laugh. "I'm so not."

She starts walking back to the house and I catch up to her so I can walk at her side, holding branches out of her way. I want to do everything I can to take the load off her.

"How did you wind up working at this place?" I ask.

"Oh, I answered a job ad. I was real smart." Her voice is laced with sarcasm.

"What do you mean?"

"Well, I should've asked a bunch more questions before I made the five-hour bus journey here. Like, *are you planning to dump the kids with me and run off?*"

"Wait, you came all that way to take the job?"

"Yeah." She flicks me a glance. A quick flash of her pale face which quickens my pulse. "I got laid off just after Christmas. Unexpectedly. And there were no other jobs where I was. So, I had to leave." She says it matter-of-factly, without any self-pity. I admire her strength even more.

"What about your family? Couldn't you stay with them?"

"Oh, I don't have any family. I'm flying solo."

My breath catches. She's alone in the world, just like me. But ten times as vulnerable.

"Did they die?" I blurt out.

She's silent for a long time.

"I'm sorry. I shouldn't have asked."

"It's okay, I'm just not used to talking about it." She clears her throat. "My mom abandoned me when I was three. I think she might've OD'd, but no one's ever told me the truth. Then I got passed around a bunch of relatives until I was sixteen, and old enough to escape. I've been on my own ever since."

"I'm so sorry, Zoe," I say, and my heart breaks for her.

"Thanks for saying so." She flashes me a small, brave smile.

Protectiveness pours through me. When she's mine, she'll never fly solo again.

We reach the gate.

"I padlocked it behind me, just in case." She takes out the key from her pocket and wrestles with the lock.

"Here, let me."

When I reach out to take it from her, her soft fingers

brush mine, and there's a jolt, like an electrical charge shooting through me.

"Oh," she says at the same moment, her head snapping toward me. I gaze deep into her eyes. They're wide and shocked. She felt it too.

It's the mate-bond. I've heard about it before. You connect body and soul, become a single energy source. I remember elders in my clan saying it was physically painful to be apart from their mate. All I know is I'd give anything to feel that electricity again.

We slip through the gate and I lock it behind us. My beast calms now that she's welcoming me into her space.

"Do you know the family?" she asks as we trek up the snowy driveway.

"No, this house has been empty for a long time. The family only moved in a couple of days ago, and I figured it was a property they inherited or something."

"So, they arrived here, dumped their kids with a brand-new employee, and left. Interesting."

I was just thinking the same thing myself. "What do you know about these kids?"

"Well, they're the wildest ones I've ever met," she says with a laugh. "They did warn me about that in the ad, at least. But what do you mean?"

I was hoping she might know about shifters already. There are a lot of us around here. That's why I made this forest my home. But where she came from—maybe they're not so common.

She doesn't pick up on my cues though. Doesn't

matter. I'm gonna prove to her that she needs to be with a shifter. This shifter.

"I meant, do you know if they have any special requirements?"

She lets out a long sigh. "From the very little their mom told me, no. They're not easy kids, but I'm guessing they haven't had a lot of discipline. Maybe not a lot of love either." She puts so much to emotion into the sentence, so much longing and pain. And suddenly, I understand something: she's talking about herself, too.

I want to take her into my arms and hug all her suffering away. Show her I'll always protect her, no matter what.

"I'm sure they'll get all they need from you," I say.

She startles. "Why do you say that?"

"It's just a feeling I get about you. I can tell you've got a big heart. And you're responsible, too."

She smiles, like she's glad to hear my words. "To be honest, I feel like I have no idea what I'm doing."

"Oh, you're doing great, trust me."

"How so? I feel like I've made one mistake after another."

"Well, if you were a different kind of person, you could just walk out right now. Leave a message with the parents. Call the cops or child protective services, whatever, and go back to where you came from. And I wouldn't even blame you."

"Oh, I couldn't abandon them now," she says, sounding shocked.

My chest warms, and I fall for her a little bit more. Shit, it's so soon. I only met her a few hours ago, and already, I can feel my heart opening to her. I thought it was a little frozen thing sitting in my chest, only big enough to keep the blood pumping around my body. But now I feel it swelling every time I so much as look at her.

"So," she says, unlocking the front door. "I left them wrapped in blankets on the couch, watching an old Christmas movie. I wonder what's going to greet us..." She pauses, lips parted. "It's quiet. No crying or screaming..."

She tiptoes into the house and I take her cue. She leads me to the living room and we peer through the open door. Three sets of shining dark eyes are glued to the TV.

She lays a hand on her chest. "Thank goodness," she whispers. Then she leads me through the house and down a set of stairs to the basement. There's the furnace, sitting cold and dark in the corner of the room.

I frown. "Your new bosses didn't start it up for you?"

"Nope. They couldn't get away from here fast enough."

Fury crackles through me. Those irresponsible pricks. How could they leave Zoe alone like this? How could they dump the kids they're supposed to be looking after?

I remember the dweeby little guy who appeared on my porch. A spineless toad, ready to piss his pants at the sight of me. I should've ripped him apart when I had the chance.

What the hell is their deal? I don't want to freak Zoe out by mentioning it just yet, but something doesn't fit quite right. A pair of humans looking after three shifter cubs. They're somebody's kids. But whose?

I try to start up the furnace, but nothing happens.

"Sure hope there's a toolbox here," I mutter.

Zoe springs into action right away, hunting around the shelves of crap. I love how she's so practical, so switched on.

Before long, we find an old metal box with a bunch of tools inside, and I get to work. I've fixed a couple of furnaces before. I used to do all kinds of jobs when I was younger—when I was still trying to be a part of the human world. In a few minutes, there's a big rushing sound and an orange flame flares. "It's connected to the water tank, so there should be hot water in about ten minutes' time," I say.

"Oh, thank you *so* much." Zoe clasps her hands together. "You're the best."

My beast swells inside me. *She says you're the best. The one.*

I shove it back down.

It's just a figure of speech, I tell it. But the truth is, I'm hungry for every little compliment she gives me, every sign she might like me. She's looking up at me, eyes shining, as beautiful as an angel. It's costing me everything I've got not to take her into my arms and kiss her senseless.

"You're welcome," I say gruffly instead.

A silence draws out between us. Need builds and builds inside me, until I can't stand it anymore. "Guess I'll be on my way now," I blurt out before I do or say something crazy.

She takes a deep breath, and I sense the thoughts spinning in that smart brain of hers.

"Would you like a hot drink?" she says.

My beast purrs in satisfaction. She was wondering whether she could trust me. And she's decided that yes, it's safe to spend a little more time with me. Her subconscious knows she's mine. I've just gotta work on the other part.

"Sounds like the best thing in the world," I say.

She blinks. It's too much, I know that. But I'm not sorry. The sooner she knows how I feel about her, the better.

I show her how to start up the furnace if it packs up again, then we go back up the stairs.

But before we've even gotten to the top of the stairs, we hear screaming.

"Oh no!" she exclaims, heading for the den at a run.

The kids are busy beating the crap out of each other. They're making all kinds of feral growls and snarls, and they look like they're one step away from shifting. I wonder if they've had their first shift yet. If it happens in front of Zoe, it'll scare the hell out of her.

"Kids, quit fighting!" Zoe yells. "Todd, Jace, Mari!" She calls each of them by name. But they don't hear her; they're intent on their rough and tumble.

I clap my hands together. "Settle down now," I say.

They spring apart, guiltily, staring at me with big, shocked eyes. They know.

That's why one of them came looking for me earlier. He was drawn to his own species. He's the one on the left, who's looking at me with recognition growing in his fierce little eyes.

Zoe flashes me a grateful look.

"Now, what's the problem?" I say.

"Todd keeps telling me what's gonna happen next!" the little girl wails. "And I just want to enjoy the story."

"I can see that would be annoying," I say. "Todd why don't you quit and just let your sister enjoy herself?"

"I'm just real *excited*!" he says, shaking his little fists with pent-up emotion.

I fight back a smile. "I hear you, little guy. But you gotta let people have their own experiences. You understand?"

"Sometimes it's real nice watching someone make their own discoveries," Zoe chips in.

He lets out an epic sigh. "I *guess*."

We share a fleeting look. The kind of look that makes my heart beat faster.

"So can you all sit here quietly, while we go in the kitchen for a minute?" she asks, making her face stern.

"Yes," they say in unison.

"YOU'VE REALLY GOT a way with them," Zoe says, as I follow her into the kitchen. While she fills up the kettle, I gaze at her lovely rear view. The soft, chocolate-brown curls bouncing on her shoulders, the perfect round curve of her ass.

She's feeling bad about herself. Like she's not good at controlling them, I think. I'm longing to tell her it's because I'm a shifter, and they react to me instinctively.

"Just good luck," I say at last. "They're bound to test you."

"They don't test *you*, though."

"Probably because I look like a crazy wild man," I say, with a laugh. She looks me up and down boldly. She's been sneaking a bunch of glances at me when she thinks I'm not looking, but this is the first time she's looked at me openly. Her mouth opens and closes again, and I sense questions forming on the tip of her tongue.

"You're wondering what I'm doing, living out in the wilderness?"

Her cheeks pink, making her look even prettier. "Kinda."

She turns away again and makes the tea. "You're like a real mountain man, right? All cut off from society."

"You thought we only existed in books, huh?"

"Yeah." There's a hint of mischief in her smile.

I take a big breath in and release it slowly. I'm not used to talking about my family. Not sure if I ever will be.

Her smile drops. "Something happened, didn't it?"

"What do you mean?"

"Something hurt you."

I go still, panic beating through me. How did she know?

Because mate, my beast reminds me.

Of course. She senses it because she's my mate.

"I lost my family, all of them at the same time, when I was young—" I break off, shove my hands in my pockets. The next sentence is hard. "I felt like I didn't deserve to be alive. I was always asking myself how come I was

the one who survived, when they were all such good
people." I clench every muscle in my body, working to
keep my feelings under control. "So, I've lived by myself
ever since."

"As penance," she says quietly.

Damn. She gets me. I thought there wouldn't be
another soul in the world who could understand me.
But here she is. *My mate.*

I gaze at her in wonder. Too darn head-over-heels to
hide my feelings.

"You're a good man," she says.

I stiffen. "You sure about that?" I say, partly because I
really want her to tell me again.

"Yeah, very." She frowns. "My boss warned me to
stay away from you. Right before they walked out on
me and their kids." She rolls her eyes.

"Well, he may not be the best judge of character."

"You met him?"

"Yup. He came to my cabin unannounced." I hesitate.
I need to be open with her, so she knows she can trust
me. "He had a problem with the fact that I was naked on
my own property. And I chased him off."

"Oh—" She claps a hand over her mouth and
giggles.

I was worried she'd be horrified at the thought. But
when she looks at me again, her pupils are dilated and
that flush in her cheeks has spread to her chest. It's
goddamn beautiful.

"Think a guy's got a right to be naked on his own
property," she says.

"Too right," I say. Ninety-nine percent of my attention is focused on the way her eyes are running all over me. On the fact she's thinking about me naked.

She takes a step forward. And another one. And suddenly, I'm dragging her into my arms.

I've never touched a woman before, but my instinct takes over. I tilt her back in my embrace and press my mouth against hers. Holy hell. It's the softest thing I've ever felt. She lets out a little moan, and her sweet, pretty lips glide against mine.

Fuck. She's not freaking out rejecting me, but she's kissing me, too. Her arms lift up and wrap around my neck, and I'm lost. I run my hands over her hair, her shoulders, while I kiss her deeper. When I feel her lips part for me, I plunge my tongue in. My beast is taking over. It's pushing at my skin, desperate to mate her.

I back her up against the counter, possessing her sweet mouth like I want to possess all of her. This girl is mine. My cock is rock hard, straining to get to her, to plunge inside her little pussy—

Yaaooowww!

A spine-tingling screech comes from the living room and we jerk apart.

She touches her finger to her lips, wonderingly.

Take her, my beast growls inside me.

We listen, but the kids have fallen silent again.

Can I? My fingers tingle, desperate to pull her into my arms again.

She gives herself a little shake. "Need to cook dinner. The kids must be starving."

"Yeah, of course," I say, disappointment washing over me.

"Maybe you can stay for dinner—?"

I shake my head. My cock is fit to burst and my beast is burning my skin. No way can I sit down to dinner and act all civilized when she's gotten me all stirred up like this.

"No, I'm good," I grunt, then cringe at the feral sound of my voice.

"I'll let you out of the gate."

"No need." I can feel my fur sprouting on my chest and the back of my neck. I've gotta get out of here before something awful happens. I charge out of the house and down the snowy driveway, bearing down on my beast with everything I've got.

5

Zoe

I wake with a start. It's still dark outside, but I set my alarm to go off at seven a.m., because kids are early birds—or so the handbook says. They're all sleeping next door. I wasn't sure what to do about sleeping arrangements. I *was* thinking about having them in the room with me, but the book says no, in no uncertain terms. I need to set boundaries, especially with challenging children. So, I put them all in the same room. I figured that however much they fight, they need to be together. They've been dumped here with a strange lady, and all they've really got is each other.

The bedrooms are pretty rundown, but I did my best to make the kids comfy, with lots of blankets and pillows, and I swapped out the broken bulbs in the table lamps.

I blink in the unfamiliar gloom, listening.

It's quiet. I hope they'll sleep a while longer.

I stretch out luxuriously, grateful that it's warm under the blankets.

I wonder if Lock is still asleep.

There I go, thinking about him again.

Well, it's not my fault after the way he kissed me yesterday.

I'd been daydreaming about it happening ever since I saw him sitting outside his cabin, looking up at the sky, all deep and thoughtful.

And then it did. And it was the most incredible moment of my life.

Those soft, hungry lips burning mine. That mountain man beard of his chafing my skin. Those big, rough hands holding me so tight.

He made me feel wild—like him. Like I wanted to just let go, throw myself at him.

If the kids hadn't been there, I would've let it all happen.

I imagine sneaking into his cabin now.

Just going down there, and creeping through the door while he's still in bed. Does he sleep naked? I bet he does.

That big muscly body all sprawled out, his mountain man cock on display.

I bet he's got a big, thick cock, to match the rest of him.

Fuck, the thought of him naked… think my panties are wet already. Weird, I've never really been a sex person. Never been that into guys. But this feeling for Lock—

It's something else. Every time I look at him, I start tingling.

I'd strip off my clothes and walk in there naked. No man has seen me naked before, and I want Lock to be the first. I imagine his cock getting bigger and bigger at the sight of me.

Then he'd just pounce on me, and take me. Make me his—

"Get off me, Jace!" comes a shrill voice from next door.

Oof... annd my hand is in my pajama pants. I tear it out, cheeks burning.

Look what he's doing to me. I've never even touched myself before.

The yelling continues. I leap out of bed and fling open the door to the kids' bedroom.

They are all on Mari's bed, wrestling.

For a moment, I stand frozen, impressed and horrified at the same time. They're going hard. Like three tiny MMA fighters. I didn't know kids that young could be so coordinated. So *brutal*.

Then I come to my senses and clap my hands together. Three heads snap in my direction.

"What on earth are you doing to each other?" I wail.

Todd releases Jace's neck from a chokehold. "Just waking up." He shrugs.

I scan each of them anxiously. They still have the right number of limbs. No one is bleeding. "Anybody hurt?" I say uncertainly.

They disentangle themselves and sit down, side-by-side, staring at me.

"You all okay?"

"We're fine, Zoe," says Mari. "We just like to have a little rough and tumble sometimes. It's nothing to worry about."

I blink at the adult tone in her voice. That's new. "Well, I'm sure your parents wouldn't see it that way."

"They don't care," Jace says.

Oh, shit. These poor things. So young, but they already understand that their parents are not the people they should be. My heart aches for them.

"Well, I care," I say, injecting brightness into my voice. "And I'd really like it if you didn't all end up black and blue while I'm taking care of you. Okay?"

"We'll be sure not to permanently injure each other," Mari says, flashing me a patient smile.

Well. I feel more unsettled than ever. There's something very unusual about these kids.

"Okay, are you old enough to get dressed by yourselves?"

"I am," Mari says. "But I usually help the other two."

And looks like she's been forced to be a carer for Todd and Jace.

"That's gonna be my job from now on," I tell her.

"Thank you," she says, and for the first time, she gives me a real smile.

It's not easy getting the twins dressed, not least because I've had very little experience of dressing other people. But a lot of wriggling and complaining later, and they're dressed in identical PAW Patrol sweatsuits.

"All right!" I yell, clapping my hands together. I'm figuring out that an energetic attitude is the best way to keep them engaged. "Who's gonna help me make breakfast?"

To my surprise, all three of them shout, "me!" and they charge toward the stairs.

"What do you kids normally have in the mornings?" I open the cupboard doors. Thank goodness the kitchen is well stocked, at least. I pull out a bunch of cereal boxes. "These?"

"I guess," Jace says, looking unimpressed.

"Don't you normally have cereal?"

"Yeah." Todd shrugs.

"But you'd prefer something else?"

"Is there any meat?" Mari asks.

"Yeah, I think so." I open the fridge, remembering I saw some sausages yesterday. There's some bacon, too. And eggs. Now I've gotten their attention. They're gathered around the fridge, practically salivating.

I take out all the rashers of bacon and put them in the skillet. The three of them get real active, hurtling around the kitchen.

"Guys, no running in the kitchen, it's not safe." I glance at them over my shoulder. They're like three lively puppies who need to burn off some energy.

I peer through the window. The gate is still chained shut, just like Lock left it last night when he vaulted over the gate in a maneuver worthy of a superhero.

"On second thoughts," I say. "Maybe you could go play in the yard for a while?"

"Yeah!" they chorus.

I spin around, give all three of them are serious look. "I want you to play sensibly and stay out of danger. You understand?"

They nod solemnly. I wrestle them into their winter coats and hats, and unbolt the front door. The second they're released, they sprint across the fresh snow, yelling joyously. I swear they are the liveliest kids I've ever seen in my life, times ten.

I've got a good view of them through the kitchen window as I prepare the breakfast. I set a bunch of timers—because multitasking has never been my strong suit—and start cooking. They're playing tag, apparently. Chasing each other through the deep snow, while snarling and growling like a trio of tiny beasts. I can't help smiling. I'm glad to see them happy after all they've been through.

I'm just taking the sausages off the grill, when the three of them scamper toward the front-left corner of the yard. I dump the sausages on a plate and crane my neck to see what they're looking at.

They are yelling something that sounds a lot like "Lock". Is he there? *Crap.* My stupid heart is beating faster. I lean forward and press my face against the window to see better.

Holy shit. That's not Lock—it's a huge brown bear!

It's a couple of yards away from the fence, and some-how, that's not terrifying but exciting to these three kids.

My heart quits fluttering and jumps into my throat. I hammer on the window. "Kids, come back here!"

If they hear me, they don't give any sign.

Then Mari starts climbing the fence. What the hell? I take one desperate look to make sure nothing is about to catch fire, and *run.*

There's not a single sensible thought in my head as I fly across the snowy yard. The only thing screaming in my brain is, *get the kids back!*

Oh my God, all three of them have scaled the fence and are scrambling down the other side.

"Todd, Jace, Mari, get back here!" I scream.

But they pay me no attention at all. They're absolutely fixated on the bear. They think he's a cuddly cartoon character or something. They seem to have no idea that it's a full-grown grizzly with massive fangs. "He's dangerous! He could eat you alive!" I holler, my throat raw.

As if in slow motion, Mari drops down to the ground and scampers towards the bear.

There's no way I'm going to get over the fence. I dash for the front gate instead. I fumble the padlock open and burst through, then look around in a panic. I need some kind of weapon. I spot a fallen branch. I snatch it up, then I run at the bear, brandishing it threateningly and screaming my lungs out the whole time.

Then I stop dead.

There are the kids, each still in one piece. There's no sign of the bear. But there's Lock—standing in the snow, buck naked.

"Come inside, there's a bear!" I scream.

Lock raises a hand. "It's okay," he calls.

"What? It's most definitely not okay. There's a huge, grizzly running around out here, and for some reason, these kids want to be eaten alive."

"Zoe, I promise you there's nothing to worry about." His voice is disconcertingly calm.

"Are you crazy? Kids, come here, please!" I'm hysterical. I think I'm even crying, and I'm definitely about to wet myself.

"C'mere." Lock hunkers down, and all three kids leap on him. Mari scrambles onto his shoulders, while the twins wrap themselves around his massive arms. "Come on, let's go." He heads back to the gate at a trot.

I follow him, head spinning. Why, why, why am I the only one who's terrified here?

The second Lock has passed through the gate, I lock the padlock again. Lock carries the kids up to the house and deposits them on the front step. I shove them through the front door. "Come in," I yell to Lock.

"Zoe, you're safe. Trust me," he says.

I stare at this naked man, standing on the front step, in absolute confusion. "How… what?" I falter. My head is spinning, and I'm using every scrap of willpower to maintain eye contact with Lock, and not steal a glance at that fire hose between his legs. But it's no use. It demands my attention. I glance at it fast. It's absolutely massive. Long and thick and dangerous looking.

When I meet his gaze again, a little smile tugs at the corner of his lips. He caught me looking.

"You're naked," I blurt out.

"Sorry." He puts his hands over his junk. "I'll go."

"No," I say forcefully. "You're going to tell me what's going on."

I see his big chest rise and fall. "How about I go put some pants on, then I'll come back and explain?"

"Yes, okay," I hear myself saying.

6

Zoe

$\mathcal{M}$ari, Jace and Todd's cheeks are glowing and their eyes are bright with excitement.

"Are you kids okay?" I ask leading them back into the kitchen.

"Yeah!" they yell boisterously. They look like they've never been better.

Trying to pretend this wasn't the weirdest half hour of my life, I crack some eggs into a skillet

"You three sit down quietly," I say sternly, and for once they obey me. I fry up the eggs, then I cook the bacon and lay it all on plates with the now-cold sausages. Not bad for a breakfast cooked amid a bear attack, I think as I dump the plates in front of the kids. Then I look up in time to see Lock striding across the yard. He's not only wearing pants, but a shirt and boots as well.

When he comes into the kitchen, despite everything, my stomach flips. He's so stupidly hot. Meanwhile, the kids, who until now have been eating like animals, drop their silverware and chant his name like he's a returning hero.

"So, you gonna tell me what the hell just happened?" I demand.

"*What* just happened?" he echoes, folding his arms and looking at me quizzically.

I force myself to stare right into those startling eyes. "You know what I'm talking about, Lock. There was a bear outside. But instead of being scared of it, the kids went crazy for it."

"He is the bear!" Todd yells.

"Just a minute, honey. Lock has something to tell us."

I fold my arms, too, drumming my fingertips against my upper arm.

He exhales slowly. "He's right. I was... I am a bear. I'm a shape shifter."

"A shape-what?"

"I'm part man, part beast. More beast than man sometimes. And I can change between my human and animal sides whenever I want."

I goggle at him. Am I dreaming? I pinch my arm. *Nope,* wide awake.

"That's why you were naked in the snow just now?" I say, once I've picked my jaw up off the floor.

"I'm real sorry about that. I wasn't planning for it to happen. I was just running in the woods and, well, their eyesight was a lot sharper than I expected. And then you came running over with that big old branch, and I was worried you were gonna take me out with it." A smile pulls at his lips.

"Stop," I say.

"I didn't want you to be scared. That's why I had to shift back. And I know this is a lot to hear."

"That's an understatement," I say.

"Had you heard of shape shifters before?"

"Yeah," I say slowly. I'd though they were a myth though.

Relief sweeps his handsome features. "I thought maybe you'd guessed that I was one."

I close my eyes for a beat. Had I? I think I knew, deep down, that he was too strong and wild and big-hearted to just be a human man. Without thinking, I raise my hand and lay it on my chest, where my heart is. I'm thinking of that pull between us. That weird electricity. When I open my eyes again, his stare is more intense than ever. I know deep in my heart that he's speaking the truth. "I-I think I sensed it, subconsciously."

A sound escapes his lips. Like a purr, but a deep, growly one. He takes a half-step closer, then his attention flickers to the kids.

"But how does Todd know you're a bear?" I say.

"Because these three kids are shifters, too. That's why they're so curious about me. How they were able to climb over the fence so easily."

I nod sagely. After what I've just heard, not much can shock me. "And their parents?"

"They're not our real mom and dad," Mari pipes up.

"What?" My head snaps toward her.

"The guy you met yesterday is human," Lock says. "So, I knew he wasn't their father."

I go over to Mari and crouch down in front of her. She stares at me with big earnest eyes. There's a weariness in her that shouldn't be there in a child that young.

"Where are your real mom and dad?" I ask.

She shrugs. "I don't know."

I glance at the twins.

"They don't know either," she says real quietly.

A burst of alarm goes through me. I get up and beckon to Lock. He follows me out of the room and shuts the door. We go to the living room.

"We need to whisper. Shifter hearing is real sensitive," he says.

"Something's not right here, is it?"

He shakes his head. "I was just thinking the same thing. Shifters don't just give their kids away to humans. They are fiercely protective of their young. Unless, maybe, their real parents died and they've been adopted by these two."

"And then just abandoned? It doesn't add up. Should I call child services or something?"

He shakes his head. "No. They're shifter kids. The usual rules don't apply."

"But what am I going to do? I'm just the hired help. What if their parents never come back?"

"Let's cross that bridge when we come to it. I'm the same species as them. I'll be able to watch out for them. Maybe even find out who they belong to."

"But for how long?"

"As long as it takes. We shifters are all connected. We are brothers. This is just like looking after my brother's kids."

"What if this was their whole plan—to dump the kids on me and run?" I pass my hand across my forehead. I feel hot and overwhelmed. And stupid. "I was so dumb to accept this job—"

"Hey!" Lock's voice is louder than before. "Don't ever say that about yourself, Zoe. You're literally the smartest person I've ever met."

He's looking at me so seriously with those mesmerizing eyes of his, goose flesh breaks out on my arms.

"And—" He hesitates, as if he's not sure whether to continue— "we shifters believe everything happens for a reason."

I frown. "You're saying I was supposed to get fired from my last job and find this one?"

His gaze darts from my eyes to my lips and back again, like he's drinking me in. "Maybe." His voice is a deep growl that goes all the way through me.

I realize how close we're standing. My nostrils are full of the scent of his skin. It's spicy, mysterious. Sexy as hell. Maybe I'm crazy, but the thought that he's half-man, half-beast is turning me on like nothing else.

He lifts his hand and cups my jaw. Then slowly, deliberately, he runs his callused thumb across my lower lip. "I think you were supposed to come here and find me, little one."

Oh, god.

I'm melting. My knees are weak, and I'm trembling

all over. I stand motionless, completely in his power, while he dips his head and kisses me.

He slides his hands into my hair and holds me still while he possesses my mouth.

He kisses me hard, hungry, plunging his tongue in deep. All I can do is cling to him. My nipples harden with a shiver and heat flares in my core.

I need his hand there, between my thighs. I imagine him working those thick fingers inside me.

As if he read my mind, he slides his hand down and cups my pussy through my jeans. "So ripe, so ready for me," he growls against my lips.

I go still. It sounds so wrong. But so *right*??

I can feel that I'm wet already... annnd... I'm grinding against his hand.

Crap. How embarrassing...

And now his hand is sliding down the front of my jeans.

I should stop him. The kids are only two rooms away.

His thick fingers slide past my waistband, and... I stifle a cry as he touches my bare pussy for the first time.

He lets off another one of those deep, growly purrs.

"Are you wet for me, little one?" he rasps.

"Yes—" my voice comes out as a gasp, because he's sliding his finger up and down my slit, getting closer to my entrance with every stroke.

"Fucking beautiful," he growls.

And he takes his hand away.

I bite back a sound of disappointment.

"I'll put a word out among the shifters I know," he says, still holding me close. "See if anyone's missing some kids."

"Thank you," I manage to say.

As I step away from him, he drags me back into his arms and gives me one more fierce kiss. "Soon," he growls. "Soon, I'll make you mine."

7

Lock

I'm carrying a tray of hot chocolates through the front door, when I pause and take in the incredible vision that greets my eyes.

Zoe is in the yard with the kids, helping them make a snowman. Her cheeks are glowing and she looks prettier than ever. Being outdoors sure suits her.

Turns out the kids have never made a snowman before, and when Zoe heard that, she looked real sad, then she promised she'd help them make the best one ever.

It's not easy because fights keep breaking out between the kids. They've just never learned how to share, Zoe told me. They all wanted to build their own individual snowman, but she encouraged them to work together instead. Now Mari has agreed to let Todd sit on her shoulders so he can reach up higher. That's real progress.

I can't believe how good Zoe is with them, so sensitive to their needs. She's gonna be the best mom in the world.

I can't wait to make her pregnant. Fill her belly with my young, and experience every part of it—from seeing our little cub for the first time, to watching it grow up, day by day.

Just as soon as I impregnate her.

My cock springs to attention again.

She's mine now.

I told her about my bear, and she didn't freak out. No, she let me kiss her again. Touch her pussy. I knew she wanted me, but I didn't really *believe* it until I felt how wet she was. Felt her tight little entrance spasming around my fingertip.

How am I gonna control myself now?

My bear is in a panic. It's worried some other beast is gonna find her and try to claim her. I know where it's coming from. There's not a beast out there who wouldn't want to make Zoe his. But there's no way I'm letting any of them come within a mile of her. Still, it won't be calm until I sink my cock into her tiny virgin pussy and give her my mark.

Zoe turns her head. Is she looking for me?

She is.

When she catches sight of me, she gives me a smile so beautiful, my chest aches.

Three little sets of nostrils are already snuffling eagerly as I bring the tray over.

"Hot chocolate!" Mari exclaims.

I hand over the mugs. I like making the kids happy, but Zoe's sound of pleasure when she buries her face in a huge mug is pure bliss.

"Delicious," she says, and my heart soars.

"Hey, you've got—" I reach out to brush a fleck of foam off her lip.

"Awww!" Mari coos.

Sheesh, that kid's too smart for her own good.

"Whaddya think?" Zoe asks, rapidly changing the subject.

"That's the biggest snowman I've ever seen." I rub my chin thoughtfully. "But it looks more like a... a..."

"A bear!" Jace yells delightedly.

"Yeah, that's what I was thinking," I say.

Jace's eyes get huge. "That's okay, right?" he says.

"Yeah, it's okay to talk about shifters in front of me and Zoe," I tell him, rubbing his tousled brown hair.

Zoe and I draw away and let the kids get back to their work.

"Someone obviously explained about shifters and told them not to tell humans about it," I whisper to her.

"So, they were raised by shifters until they were old enough to talk, at least?" she replies.

I feel the warmth of her sweet breath in my ear. It takes all my self-control not to snap my head around and claim her lips with my own. "Yeah. I was just thinking that."

We stand side-by-side, drinking our hot chocolates and watching Todd and Jace taking turns to stand on Mari's shoulders and work on the bear's face.

"They're so much better behaved when you're around," Zoe says.

I huff out a breath. "They're just calmer around another shifter. Guess they understand me better."

"It breaks my heart that they've been deprived of that."

"Me too. Just a good thing you answered that job ad though." I lay my hand on her arm. "I'm gonna do everything I can to find their parents, don't you worry."

She breaks into a smile. "Thank you, Lock, I appreciate that. So much."

I gather up the kids' discarded mugs and take them back to the house. I'm just loading them into the dishwasher, when I hear the sound of Zoe's footsteps. She tears off her jacket and woolly hat, and her long brown curls come tumbling out.

I'm still straightening up when she runs into my arms. She loops her arms around my neck and pulls me down for a kiss. My heart pounds as I lean in and possess her small, sweet mouth again. Her lips are cold on the outside, while her tongue is like warm velvet.

When I press her curvy little body against me, my cock turns rock-hard again, jabbing against her belly. Trying to get to her.

"I want you so bad," I growl against her lips. I'm close to losing control.

"You do?"

"You have no idea. You're so sexy. That sweet virgin sense of yours is driving me crazy."

"Oh, you know?" she says in a high, tight voice. She's too precious. She has no idea how compelling her scent is to a beast like me. I'm one step away from yanking her jeans down and taking her right over the counter. But, no. I'm gonna make darn sure her first time is as perfect as she is. Who knows how that's gonna happen with the kids around, but I'm determined not to rush things, no matter how my beast is tearing me up inside.

Reluctantly, I pull away from her. "I've got to go out, run a couple of errands," I tell her. "Will you be okay with the kids?"

She peers through the window. "Yeah, I think they're about done outdoors, and it's getting kinda cold. I'll keep them inside."

"Yeah, you do that. Lock the doors and don't let anyone in, but me."

"I won't," she says with a grin. I wonder if she's thinking how cozy we sound. Like we're already together. Mated. What a beautiful thought.

I give her one more kiss goodbye, then I head over to my old truck, which is parked up in a clearing a half mile from my cabin.

It kills me being apart from her. But being the beast I am, I don't even own a cell phone, so I've gotta do what I've gotta do in person.

And when I'm back, I swear I'm never letting her out of my sight again.

8

Zoe

The giant snow bear is complete at last. And by some miracle, the kids are finally unbounced. They are gazing at their creation in quiet awe.

"You guys, this is the best snowman I've ever seen in my entire life," I tell them.

"Really?" Todd asks with such earnestness my heart melts.

"Hand on heart." I press my hand to my chest. "Come on, let's take some photos."

The afternoon sunlight is glinting off the snow, and it's a perfect wintry scene. I take a bunch of selfies and shots of the three of them gathered around the snow bear. When I'm done, they rush over and stare at my phone screen curiously. They're not used to seeing themselves, I gather from their comments. No one's ever taken photos before? That's one of the saddest things I've heard.

When we're all selfied out, we go inside, and I lock the door, just like Lock told me to. I love the way he was taking charge like that, like we were a real couple. Could that happen?

We're different species, but I want to be with him.

Sure, I want him so bad it hurts. But I also want to just spend time with him, get to know all about him. He makes me feel like I can open myself up to him. And I've never felt like that with anyone before.

Shit, it's so soon, but I think I might be falling for this big, sexy bear-man.

The kids are yawning and drowsy. I tug their coats off, then I put them on the couch while I go make some warm milk and grab a plate of cookies. When I come back, they're piled together like puppies. While they're munching, I go hunt down a bunch of blankets in the bedroom closet. When I come back, the other two are sleeping, but Mari is staring at me with her solemn black eyes.

"Will you and Lock be our mom and dad now?" she whispers.

I frown, not sure how to answer. "You have your own parents, honey," I say at last.

She looks at me seriously. "They are never coming back, you know?"

"W-what do you mean?"

Her eyes get very bright. "I shouldn't have said that," she mutters, "because now you'll leave."

My heart breaks for this poor little girl.

"Mari, I will never leave you until I know you're safe. I can promise you that."

She closes her eyes in a very adult expression of relief.

"You said that Michelle and Adrian weren't your real parents. What makes you say that?" I ask cautiously. But she doesn't reply.

She's not asleep. I can see a little spasm in her eyelids. Either she doesn't know, or she doesn't want to tell me, poor thing.

WHILE THEY'RE SNOOZING, I decide to get the house in some kind of order. I track down a bunch of cleaning supplies and get to work.

I don't mind cleaning, especially when I've got Lock to daydream about.

An hour and a half later, and I've made a whole lot more progress than I'd expected. It's actually a nice house, under all that dust and grime. I get the sense that it's owned by an older person who's maybe gotten less active over the years. A lot of the furnishings are outdated and real worn. There are four bedrooms though, and I wonder if it used to be a family house, full of fun and laughter.

The last bedroom along the hallway is full of cardboard boxes. Some of them are open and I see a bunch of files peeking out.

I hesitate in the doorway. I don't have the right to

look at any of this stuff, but I need to figure out what's going on.

With a sigh, I grab the nearest box and start rifling through.

A few minutes later, I strike gold. There's a ton of mail that's been sent to this property, addressed to a Mr and Mrs Wilson.

Then I find the deeds to the house. Yup, they are—or were—the legal owners. They've owned it for forty-seven years.

I head back downstairs. The kids are still sleeping. I settle down on a battered old armchair and pull my phone out of my pocket.

There's a text from an unknown sender:

Is everything ok at home? I've been thinking about you a lot x

My heart jumps.

Lock.

He must've bought a phone. I read the words over and over.

at home.

He's thinking of this place as *our* home. Mine and his and the kids. My stomach is full of butterflies. I feel like I've just stepped into my deepest, most unacknowledged fantasy. I tap out a reply:

Kids are snoozing :) I'm doing some research. Me too xx

I hit send. Then I regret not having the guts to say a whole lot more. But these words don't come easy for me. This heart of mine has been locked shut for a long, long time.

The phone pings again.

Can't wait to get back to you, baby.

Oh, god.

I press the phone to my chest, imagining him saying those words in his growly voice.

Same :) My thumbs tap out my flimsy reply.

Darn, he deserves more than that.

I'm really looking forward to seeing you, I manage, blushing all the while.

"Okay, back to work," I mutter, tapping my internet app.

I find out that John and Mary Wilson are both deceased, and the house is still in their names. A couple with their names also had a child named Adrian.

My heart is beating faster. I feel like I'm a big step closer to tracking them down.

I shove my phone back in my pocket, aware that it's getting late. The kids are waking up, yawning extravagantly and rubbing their fists in their eyes.

I clap my hands together. "Hey, you guys, why don't you go grab some toys, and bring them down here to play with?"

While they're gone, I plug in a little device that I just found in a box of stuff in their room.

It switches on. It's a baby monitor, and there's an app to connect it up with my phone.

I go into the kitchen, and my phone screen displays the three of them romping around the living room.

"Gamechanger," I mutter. Things just got a lot easier. I prop my phone on the counter, and get to work figuring out what I'm going to cook.

I'm just folding some spaghetti into a bubbling pan

of water when I hear the sound of a vehicle approaching.

My stomach does a triple flip.

Is it ridiculous that I'm so excited to see him?

I can't help myself; I rush to front door and tear it open. At the same moment, all three kids stream past me and launch themselves at Lock, shrieking in excitement.

Daddy's come home, I think, and startle.

Where did *that* come from?

"Hey, kids!" Lock exclaims. He picks them up one by one and hugs them tight, before pressing his forehead to theirs. Their animals are connecting, I realize as calm transforms Jace's features. Being with him is doing them so much good.

Then Lock puts the kids down and turns to me. There's such fire in his gaze, it knocks me sideways. He strides toward me and draws me into his arms. He holds my head gently against his chest, like he's cradling it, and I hear the deep, growly sound of his breathing. I'm kinda relieved that he doesn't kiss me in front of the kids. Don't think I'd be able to act normal in front of them afterwards.

"I missed you like crazy," he growls, close to my ear.

I stop breathing. "You did?"

"Big time. But I'm home now." He plants a kiss on top of my head and releases me.

Home. Every time I hear that beautiful word, I just melt. It's got nothing to do with this house, or any other place I've ever lived in. It means being with *him*.

"Better get back to the dinner," I say.

Keeping his arm around me, Lock leads me inside, and the kids scamper around us.

I serve up four big portions of spaghetti and meatballs for the hungry bears, and a smaller one for me. They all dive right in. The kids are too busy devouring their food to talk, but Lock is full of compliments on my cooking. He looks tired, with dark shadows under his eyes, which only makes him look sexier.

"How was your afternoon?" I ask.

He grins, tugging his phone out of his back pocket and dumping it on the table.

"Well, I said I'd never get one of these," he says, with a sparkle in his eyes. "But turns out it's necessary these days."

A tingle goes through me. I never thought a phone could be so romantic.

"Otherwise, I think I have some leads."

I gasp. "That's great!"

"I spoke to a few people, including someone who knows an investigator, so hopefully something will come of that."

"Thank you, so much." I shake my head, overwhelmed at how much he's done for me.

"Of course, Zoe." He frowns. "We're in this together."

WHEN WE'RE FINISHED EATING, Lock makes a fire in the living room, and we settle down to watch a movie together. The kids vote for an action movie, but, remembering this morning's MMA session, I talk them into a Pixar production instead.

Lock and I sit side by side, and Mari, Todd and Jace pile around us, as if they've done it a hundred times before.

How is it possible to feel so comfy, but so wound tight at the same time?

When the closing credits roll, I sit up and stretch.

"Okay, time to get ready for bed," I say.

"Awww!" they huff.

"Let's watch one more," Jace whines.

"You guys have had a long day."

Lock leans close and stage whispers, "If you all go upstairs and get ready real fast, I'll tell you a bedroom story. How about that?"

Two seconds later, there are no kids in sight. All I can hear is the sound of six little feet pounding up the stairs.

"Thank you," I say with a happy sigh as I pull myself up. "I'd better help them brush their teeth. I can handle the bedtime story, too."

Lock gives me a wounded look. "You kidding me? I wouldn't miss it for everything."

I break into a grin. "Are you real?"

Before I can step away, he catches my hand and presses a kiss to my lips. "You'd better believe it," he growls against my mouth.

I HUSTLE the kids through baths and teeth brushing and pajamas, and I send them through to Lock, one by one.

When I finally come into the bedroom, he's sprawled

out on Todd's bed, and the three of them are piled around him, again.

And he's not reading a story, but telling it from memory. I pause by the door, just out of sight, and listen.

It's the tale of a bear who's lost his family, and wanders around in the world until he finds his people. The kids listen spellbound, and my heart aches.

It sounds so much like my own secret dreams. And Lock's, too?

Lock keeps going with an epilogue, running it on until three pairs of eyes have started to droop.

We give each other a thumbs-up, and he helps me move Jace and Mari into their own beds.

Then we creep downstairs together.

* * *

THE MOMENT my feet hit the bottom step, Lock drags me into his arms.

We tumble through the living room door and he shuts it behind us.

At last, we're alone together.

I feel his big body quaking and sense the passion he's been holding back.

He kisses me long and deep, exploring my mouth, running his hands through my hair.

Then he draws back, cupping my face in his big, rough hands. "I'm sorry I left you alone all day, baby."

I blink. "That's okay. I'm used to being alone," I manage to say.

He gives me such a sad look. "You'll never be alone again."

He traces a line of burning kisses from my lips, to my jaw, to the hollow of my neck. "A bear looks after his mate. Puts her needs first, always."

I sigh—at the magic of his lips. At his words. He keeps going, all the way down to the top button of my shirt. I hold my breath, willing him to unfasten it. I want his touch so bad I'm ready to beg.

Suddenly, he tears himself away with a ragged groan. "I should go."

"What? Why?" I whimper, then cringe at the naked need in my voice.

He chafes my lower lip with the pad of his thumb. "Because I'm about to hit the point of no return, baby. Where I won't be able to control myself."

I swallow hard. "Maybe I don't want you to," I tell him. I close my lips around his thumb and draw it into my mouth. I don't know what I'm doing, but it feels good. I suck it a little, tasting the saltiness of his skin.

A growl of pure hunger pours from his throat.

Oh, that's sexy.

He pulls his hand away and fixes me with a serious look. "Zoe, I don't think you know what you're saying."

I take a deep breath and lift my chin. "I'm saying I need you to fuck me, right now."

9

Lock

*F*uck.

She's trembling a little, but her blue eyes are full of determination.

I pick up the scent of her arousal with every breath I take.

Desire shudders through me.

I lay my fingertips on her shoulders. "You have no idea how much I want that. But we bears don't just fuck. We mate."

"Mate?" she repeats. She's looking at me steadily, but I see the telltale dilation of her pupils. The thought of it turns her on. Shit.

"What's the difference?"

I step in a little closer, so my aching cock presses against her belly. "Well, mating is forever."

"Oh—" Her pretty lips work, trying to shape questions. "You mean, once you have sex, that's it?"

"Yup. A bear only mates his mate."

She blinks several times. "You've never mated before?"

"Nope. I never found the right girl."

"A-are you saying I'm the right girl?" She's blushing, like she's embarrassed by her words. It's totally adorable.

"Of course, Zoe. You're the one I want to spend the rest of my life with."

She gives a shocked laugh. "But how do you know? You only just met me."

I shrug. "I've seen so much of you in the last couple of days. How brave you are, how protective and caring. How vulnerable. How in need of love. But, to tell you the truth, my bear knew as soon as it laid eyes on you."

"How?"

"A shifter knows its mate. I didn't know how it was gonna feel, but now it's happened, it's obvious."

"Like… like electricity, sizzling between us?"

My breath catches in my throat. "You feel it, too, huh?"

She nods eagerly.

"Like it hurt my heart being apart from you today."

Her eyes are sparkling like starlight. "This is real, isn't it?"

"Sure is."

She loops her arms around my neck. "Okay, maybe you should show me how this mating thing works."

A growl escapes my lips and I kiss her, long and deep. "Well, first of all we get naked."

Her gaze darts to the living room door. "One second." She picks up one of the chairs that are sitting around a dining table and jams it under the door handle. Then she taps on the screen of her phone, and leaves it propped up on the chair.

"Baby monitor," she explains.

When she turns back, there's a wicked glint in her eye. "You said get naked, right?" She holds my gaze while she unfastens the top buttons of her shirt.

Fuck, she's killing me. I can't hold back anymore. I snatch her up off her feet and carry her over to the couch.

I tear at her shirt and jeans, desperate to get at her bare skin. She helps me, and the next thing I know, she's laying back on the cushions in just her underwear. I go still, feasting my eyes on her lovely big tits and thick thighs.

"Oh, I don't match." She wraps one arm across her tits, and holds her other hand over her panties, trying to hide her underwear from me.

"Looks perfect to me," I tell her, taking in those little scraps of lace which barely contain her curves. "But if you're embarrassed, we should definitely take them off."

"Ohh—" she bites her lip.

Taking that as her agreement, I snatch at her panties and yank them off in one go. A voice in my head tells me I need to go slow, but my beast forcing its way through, taking control.

Her scent is stronger now, like the sweetest nectar. I crumple her panties in my hand, raise them to my nose and *inhale*. "Fuck, you're wet," I growl.

Then I spread her thighs and look at her pussy for the first time.

She squirms in my grasp, but I hold her tight, keeping her thighs wide apart.

"Let me see it. What a pretty little thing," I mutter. "So pink and tiny."

How's my dick gonna fit in there?

I spread her lips. Her little entrance is still closed up. Soon my cock is gonna break right through it. Claim her virginity.

Mine! my beast growls.

I'm barely holding it back. All it wants is to shove inside her.

But I'm gonna go slow, make sure she's good and ready for me.

"First I'm gonna taste you," I tell her, dipping my head to her dripping-wet slit.

My beast purrs. Fuck me if she doesn't taste even sweeter than she smells. I lap up her juices like the first honey of springtime.

"Oh, god," she cries out, snatching my hair up in her fists. Her hips jolt, and she wriggles until her little bud is pressed up against my tongue. So darn sexy. When I latch onto it, she whispers my name over and over in a sweet breathy voice. "Oh, Lock, that feels so good. Please don't stop."

She sighs and pants and writhes around, getting

pleasure from my tongue. I can't wait to feel this little pussy coming around my cock. Watch her lose control.

She's already revving up. I hear her breathing faster, feel her hips making little jerks.

I tear myself away.

She stares at me quizzically.

"I need to be inside you," I tell her.

A mischievous smile tugs at her lips. "But you're not even naked yet."

I can't resist a grin. "Good point." I tear off my clothes, and immediately feel more like myself. I'm never totally at ease when I'm dressed.

"Better—?" I start to say. Then I catch her expression. Her cheeks are flushed and she's looking *kinda terrified*. I follow her gaze, all the way to my cock, which is jutting out and swollen like never before.

"It's real big," she mutters.

"Uh—" I grasp it with my hand, encircle the thick shaft. "I guess so."

Her nostrils flare. "Don't think it's gonna fit inside me."

"Of course, it will. It was made for you, baby."

"Because I'm your mate?"

"Yup. Here—" I arch over her, thinking she'll be less intimidated when she sees it up close. I take her hand and press it to my dick.

And I swear I almost come on the spot. Didn't realize her hand would feel that darn good. I close my eyes to stop them rolling back in my head.

"Oh—" she murmurs. "It's hot, and so *hard*. But silky on the outside."

"Uh huh," I grunt through gritted teeth. Before I know it, she's stroking my aching shaft.

Fuck.

She's awkward at first, but then she gets more confident. I see her watching me, trying to figure out what I like.

She's still wearing her bra. While she works my dick, I push it right down and free her tits.

Holy hell, they're beautiful. Big and creamy, with tender pink nipples. When I squeeze them, she moans. I've gotta taste them, too. I move down her body and take them into my mouth, one then the other. She sighs in pleasure and wraps her thighs around my waist.

Then she wriggles underneath me, and now my cock is pressing up against the top of her soft thigh. She's so wet, I can feel her juices running out of her.

Fuck, she's ready for this.

"You need me inside you?" I growl.

"Uh huh." Her voice is strained.

I press my cock against her wet, swollen pussy. "Ready for me to fuck you?" I slide it up and down her slit.

She pants and bucks her hips. I keep pushing at her entrance, wanting it to open for me.

"Fuck, Lock…" she wraps her arms around me, gripping me tight.

I push in, just the head.

"Oww…fuck…" she curses. She keeps ahold of me though. "Give it to me, Lock," she mutters.

Claim her, my beast roars. It surges in me and I shove

all the way in. Every inch of my monster dick forces its way into her tiny pussy, breaking through her virginity.

She squirms and whimpers, but I don't quit until it hits home.

Her mouth falls open and she stares up at me, all shocked. "It's in me, isn't it?" she gasps out.

"Yeah that's right. Deep in your little pussy."

I slide in and out, just a little bit. Her pussy feels hot and torn, and it's gripping me so tight, my dick is pulsating.

"Hurts—" Her nails dig into me. "Oh...wait..." Her fingers relax their grip on my back.

I grin. "That feel good?"

"Yeah." Her head falls back against the couch cushions and I watch the emotions shifting across her beautiful face. "Don't stop."

With a roar, I unleash my desire. My hips thrust and my dick pounds into her, over and over. My mate. The most beautiful, incredible girl in the world. Filling her up, stretching out her little virgin pussy.

She's mine, she's mine, I think with every thrust.

I feel feral, beastly, but she keeps her gaze on me, staring right into my eyes. She accepts me, all of me.

We're moving in perfect rhythm, her hips bucking, meeting my surging cock. We're so opposite—me so savage and rough, and her so delicate and perfect, but somehow we complement each other. Creating something beautiful from this wild mating.

"Oh, wow, something's happening..." she cries out.

"Yeah, that's it, come around my dick," I growl. I give three hard thrusts, and it happens.

It's like she just detonated around my cock. Her back arches and her pussy spasms and spasms around me, while she cries out in ecstasy. I keep going, wanting to stretch out that beautiful moment for as long as possible.

Her pussy is milking me, drawing out my seed. My beast rises up. It's time.

Now! Claim her.

I feel my razor-sharp canines bust through my jaws. I don't want to hurt her, but it's gotta happen. I bite down on the tender flesh on the side of her neck.

"Oww!" she cries out. But she doesn't pull away. Instead, she goes soft, relaxing into it. She knows what's happening.

As my canines break through her skin, my seed pours out of me like liquid fire. Shooting into her fertile young womb.

"Oh, Lock—" Her nails tear into my back and she comes again, her little pussy spasming around my ejaculating cock. Fucking beautiful. Couldn't have been more perfect if I'd dreamed it up.

When she finally collapses back against the cushions, I pull out real slow, but she still makes a face.

"I'm sorry if I hurt you, baby," I say, gathering her up into my arms. I pull a blanket over us, checking she's warm enough.

"That's okay. You took my virginity," she says, and breaks into a grin. Then she frowns and fingers her neck. "Think you did something else, too?"

"Mmm… I gave you my mark."

"What's that?"

"It shows every other beast that you're my property."

"Oh… Is that gonna be there forever?"

"Uh huh."

"I like that." She snuggles even closer and my chest warms.

Of course, she does, because she's my mate.

10

Zoe

I wake up on the couch, wrapped up in blankets. It's still dark and Lock is standing in front of the fire, adding some more logs to the embers. He tried to take me up to bed at some point, but something tells me I'm not going to be able to keep quiet when he's fucking me. So, it's better for all concerned if we stay down here.

There's just enough room for both of us if we snuggle really close. Luckily, that's exactly what I want to do with my big, growly mate. For the first time in my life, I fell asleep with a man's arms around me. Protecting me, keeping me safe.

Is that how things are going to be from now on? I wonder. Then I remember Lock's teeth sinking into my neck.

My heart gives a little jump. I'm mated to a big grizzly bear shifter. It seems incredible, but so right, somehow.

"What time is it?" I mutter when Lock straightens up.

He bounds over to me. "Good morning, baby. It's seven-thirty." The look he gives me makes me melt. He crouches in front of me, stroking my hair. "How did you sleep?"

"So well. But why are you up so early?"

"I heard my phone going. Guess what?"

"What?"

"Beau, the investigator I got put in touch with, thinks he's found the kids' real parents."

I jolt upright. "What?"

"There's a family of grizzly shifters a four-hour drive away. They both got shot by hunters, and when they came to, three of their kids were gone. A little girl and twin boys. Their names are different, but I think it's them."

I gasp. "That's amazing!"

Lock clasps my hands in his. "We've gotta drive over there."

"Yeah, let's go!" I throw the covers back.

"Whoa, not so fast," he growls.

"What?"

"Something important we've got to do first." He pushes me back down, and arches over me.

"What's that?" I say, full of innocence, as he spreads my thighs.

"It'll work better if I show you," he growls, his cock already rubbing against my pussy.

* * *

SIX HOURS LATER, we are passing a sign saying *Welcome to Twin Falls.*

"We're here," I whisper to Lock. The kids are asleep in the back of the truck. We didn't tell them where we were going, in case it doesn't work out. We just said we were going on a day trip, and that was enough for them to pile into the truck, chattering excitably.

They're really good kids. I think how much they've changed in the past couple of days. How difficult I thought they were when I first arrived. All they needed was some love and a sign that someone gave a crap about them.

As we pull off the highway and weave through some small-town streets, I hear yawning and stretching coming from behind me.

"I *know* this place," says Mari's little voice.

My breath catches. "Where from, sweetie?"

"I don't know," she says drowsily, but Lock and I exchange a glance. This feels like *something.*

We pass through an area of dense forest, then pull into a parking lot. A guy and a girl climb out of an RV— the only other vehicle parked there. He has long graying hair and a beard, and the girl is younger. She's real pretty with long, dark auburn hair and freckles.

"Howdy." He waves. "Lock and Zoe? I'm Beau and

this is Savannah." They shake our hands warmly. "And the kids?"

Right on cue, they spill out of the truck. He looks at them closely then breaks into a grin. "Yup, I'm pretty darn sure they're the ones."

I squeeze Lock's hand, bursting with excitement.

Beau and Savannah lead us through the forest on foot.

After a few minutes a guy steps out from behind a tree, and I jump.

"Who the hell are you—?" He doesn't finish the sentence. Instead, his face transforms with amazement and he lets out a ragged gasp. "Jenny?" He tears past us, and the next thing I know, Mari is in his arms.

"Daddy!" she shrieks, clinging to him tight.

"Alec, Jax, c'mere!" He beckons to the twins. They go to him uncertainly, but a moment later, all four of them are in a group hug. Then he yells over his shoulder, "Ellie, get over here. I've got something to show you."

A tall, strong-looking woman comes hurrying along the forest trail. Her face is thin and tense, but when she catches sight of the kids, she lets out a shout of joy and drops to her knees. "Oh, my babies."

"Mama!" Mari whimpers, and throws herself into the woman's arms.

"Think we found the parents," Beau says with a grin.

I look up at Lock, overflowing with gratitude. Tears are pouring down my face. He puts his arm around me and holds me close, and together we watch the beautiful reunion.

"So, not Mari, Jace and Todd, but Jenny, Alec and Jaxx," I say.

"You did real good, baby," Lock says.

"I didn't do anything. It was all you."

He crooks one of his thick eyebrows. "Are you kidding? You took the job, knowing it was gonna be difficult. You gave them more love and care than they've had in a long time. And you protected them as best you could. That's why we're here now."

I shrug. "Guess I'm not as hopeless with kids as I thought I was."

"Honey, you're a natural. Trust me."

ELLIE AND VINCE, THE KIDS' parents, invite us to their cabin. They're both crying non-stop and they can't stop thanking us. They are part of a big shifter community. Deep in the forest is a bunch of log cabins, organized around the edges of a clearing, and there are shifters milling around, some in human form, others in bear form. Most of the humans are naked, but they hurry indoors and put some clothes on when they see us approach.

"This is… amazing," I say to Lock. I'm still getting used to the fact that there's this whole other species that lives under the radar of human existence.

"It's normal." He shrugs happily. "Me, living by myself, like some crazy mountain man—that was not normal."

I squeeze his hand. "But you were hurting."

"I *was.*"

We exchange a long look. It's weird, but I'm starting to feel like I can pick up on his thoughts. Whenever we lock eyes, I somehow hear his voice in my head. Right now, he's telling me he stopped hurting the moment I walked into his life.

Same here. I think the thought real hard. A second later, Lock breaks into a smile.

"You heard that, right?"

"Course," he says, like it's the most natural thing in the world.

INSIDE THE FAMILY HOME, Ellie and Vince make hot drinks for us all, and we sit down and debrief, while the kids cling to their parents like they never want to let them go again. Ellie explains that Jenny and the twins were snatched two years ago, and they've been looking for them tirelessly, but there were no leads. Vince asks all about the abductors, his knuckles whitening as I describe what happened. I hand over the deeds of the house and all the other bits of information I've gathered about them.

"I can help you track them down," Beau offers.

"Whenever you're ready." Vince rolls his shoulders. He's a huge, meaty guy, but I see how much the loss of his children has broken him.

"And how about you two?" Ellie asks, pulling her long braid over her shoulder. "How long have you been mated?" I see her gaze drift to the mark on my neck and

I feel a surge of pride. Her dark eyes are kind and interested.

Lock draws me closer on the couch, and we relate our whirlwind romance, and how Mari's—uh, Jenny's—river dive brought us together.

"Thank you, all of you. I can't tell you how grateful I am for everything you've done." Ellie lays her hand on her chest with a deep sigh. "Now, can we offer you a place to stay for the night?"

Beau and Savannah explain that they have their RV, so they'll head home.

"What do you think?" Lock says close to my ear.

I look out the window. It's already dark and it's a long drive home. "We could stay, if she really means it?"

He chuckles. "She means it, trust me. Bears are real sociable. Uh, apart from me."

I grin. "I reckon you're pretty sociable. Or at least, you have potential."

* * *

THE 'PLACE TO STAY' is actually an entire vacant log cabin. Inside, it's neat and super cozy. It has a separate bedroom with a king-size bed, and Ellie brings us some fresh sheets.

"This is lovely," I say, bringing my bag in from the truck.

"Nicer than that creepy old house, huh?" Lock replies.

I wrinkle my nose. "It is a creepy house, isn't it?"

"Only because it felt sad."

"What's gonna happen when Beau tracks down the abductors?" I ask. "Will he turn them over to the cops?"

Lock's lips harden into a grim line. "Nope. They're shifter kids. They don't exist in official human records. Explaining to the cops what happened would be like tearing the lid right off our world. But don't worry, they won't get away with what they've done. We shifters solve problems our own way."

I nod. Funny, a week ago, the thought of renegade justice would've freaked me out. Now, my eyes have been opened to a whole new world, where everything I thought I knew about life and loyalty has been turned on its head.

Lock shuts the door and bolts it behind us. "Ellie says we've got an hour till dinner."

I give myself a shake, and I stop thinking about everything else. Everything but my mate, who's standing in front of me with fire in his eyes.

I cock my head. "How are we gonna entertain ourselves until then?"

"Well, I'm planning to make you come all over my cock," he growls, reaching for me.

I'm too quick for him, though. I dart away and make a dash for the bedroom.

He comes after me and catches me up, before tossing me down on the bed.

I let out a squeal. But when I see his expression, I go still. "What is it?"

His nostrils flare and I hear his bear's growly breathing.

"You know I love you, right?" he says at last.

My breath catches. "You do?"

"So much. You're so amazing, Zoe. I'm so lucky to have you."

"Oh, I love you, too," I tell him.

A groan of relief rushes from his lips.

Then he strips my clothes off.

This time it's different. Still wild and thrilling, but I feel the love pouring out of us and into each other. When his cock fills me up, I feel us truly connecting as mates.

This time, he growls that he loves me as he fills me with his seed.

* * *

DINNER IS full of laughter and happy tears. We all gather around the family's big kitchen table and Ellie ladles out massive portions of venison stew.

We've just sat down when their eldest daughter, Becky, returns from a day trip. She walks into the room and lets out a scream when she sees the little brothers and sister she thought she'd lost forever. They run into each other's arms, shrieking in joy.

Other members of the clan come around all the time, overjoyed to reunite with the kids. They thank us so many times I feel embarrassed.

"You're family now, you know that?" Lock whispers. "Like it or not."

"I like it," I tell him, happily.

* * *

THE NEXT MORNING, Ellie insists we stay for breakfast. My throat gets tight as I chat to the kids for what will be the last time. The last few days have been such a roller-coaster of emotions. Struggling so much with them at first, then daydreaming that I could keep them forever. Then taking them back home where they truly belong. They look so happy here, but I'm going to miss them a lot.

When Lock and I head back to the cabin to grab our stuff, I burst into tears.

He's right there, taking me into his arms. "What is it, baby?"

"Oh, it's silly," I protest.

He draws back and looks at me seriously. "Nothing you feel is silly, Zoe. I want to know every single one of your thoughts."

"You may regret saying that one day," I sniffle. "I'm just sad. You know, for a minute it felt like the five of us were a family. And I'm so, so glad that the kids have got their real family back, but it's just gonna take me a little while to get over it."

"I feel the same," he says, rubbing my back.

I go still. "You do?"

He shrugs. "Of course. It felt real cozy last night, all of us together. But, guess what?"

"What?"

"We'll have that with our own kids one day."

My heart gives a jump. "Kids, plural?"

"As many as I can breed out of you."

I gasp and slap his arm. "That's rude... but also kinda *sexy*?" I mutter as my clit tingles.

He pulls me closer. "You better believe it. I'm gonna breed your sweet body every day from now on, until my seed is spilling out of you."

I bite my lip. "You know, a few days ago, I was darn sure I never wanted kids."

"But now?"

"Well, I guess they're not so bad after all."

He's looking at me intently. Kinda hopeful, kinda wounded.

"I can't wait to have your kids, Lock," I tell him.

He lets out a possessive growly sound, and holds me tighter.

I gaze out of the window. "I'm gonna miss this place, too," I say.

"Why?"

"Because… it feels like home."

"Then let's stay."

"Huh?" I give him a questioning look.

"They've already offered. This place is ours if we want it."

I blink, trying to process the words. "We could live here, permanently?"

"Yup."

"Like, become part of the community?"

"Definitely. That part is not optional." He laughs.

"And we won't have to say goodbye to the kids." I exhale slowly. "B-but won't you miss your cabin?"

"Nope. I was a miserable bastard the whole time I was there. I'm ready to start a new life with you."

"Do you think the clan will accept me, you know, as a human?"

"You're already accepted. That's how bears work. If they trust you, that's it."

My heart lifts. This is about the best thing I could imagine. Why not stay here with my gorgeous shifter mate, surrounded by his own people? "Yes," I say. "Let's stay."

Lock breaks into a grin. "We're going to be so happy here, baby." Then he strides to the door and flings it open. "We're staying!" he shouts.

A chorus of whoops fills the air.

I dart over to him. The whole clan seems to be standing in front of their cabins, watching us expectantly.

"Um, were they waiting to find out?"

"Maybe," he says with a sheepish grin. When he takes me in his arms, my cheeks warm at the *awws* that greet us.

Then he kisses me and I don't think about anything else, apart from how much I love my gorgeous, protective bear mate.

EPILOGUE

One year later

"Sorry, sorry!" I call as I bustle through the front door of our cabin. "Ellie and the girls kept me talking and I couldn't get away—"

When I catch sight of Lock, I burst out laughing.

He's carrying our son, Aiden, in a sling on his chest while stirring a bunch of pots on the stove. But his hair is kinda standing on end and judging by the puce shade of Aiden's face, the baby's been grizzling for a long time. My usually easygoing mate looks *harassed*.

The eyes that meet mine are wild, but in a second, he dissolves into laughter, too.

I rush over and wrap my arms around the two of them. "You seem a little stressed, huh?"

He mumbles something about multitasking and kisses me on the lips tenderly.

I melt a little bit. Even when he's busy or over-whelmed, he takes a moment to show me how much he loves me. Then I kiss our son on his velvety forehead, inhaling his delicious baby scent at the same time. He looks just like his dad, with plenty of thick dark hair, and his eyes are already lightening to a startling emerald green. I can't believe there was a time when I didn't want kids. I fell in love with this little guy the moment he came out of me. And it seems like I have pretty good instincts for childcare. Which is just as well as it turns out a lot of the stuff in that old handbook I bought is not relevant to shifters. At three months old, Aiden can already hold his head up easily, and he's just learning to crawl.

"Let me take over cooking," I say.

"It's okay, I've got it. You take Aiden if you want."

I reach for the straps on the sling eagerly, always happy to nurse my baby.

By the time we sit down to dinner, Aiden's little belly is full, and he's drowsing contentedly. Lock is a great cook. Tonight it's Greek moussaka, and it tastes as good as it smells.

"The girls are asking when they can babysit Aiden," I say. Jenny and her big sister Becky love him. They think of him as their own little brother. Meanwhile, Alec and Jaxx can't wait for him to be old enough to join in their rough and tumble games.

I can't believe how much the kids have changed in the last year. Within a week of coming back home, they lost that watchful look they'd had, and they've each gained several pounds. It turned out the abductors had been feeding them on all kinds of crap, instead of the fresh-meat diet that shifter cubs need to grow up big and strong.

As for the abductors... well, it took Beau and Vince a couple of weeks to catch up with them. They'd fled over the country border and were hiding out in a small town, where they thought no one would ever find them. I overheard Beau telling Lock that Vince was so mad, his bear burst out of him the moment he laid eyes on them. Apparently, Beau had to stop him from ripping their throats out before he'd gotten them to confess.

Eventually, the couple admitted the whole thing— shooting Vince and Ellie, then taking the kids. Then dumping them when they got too wild and hard to manage.

I don't know what happened after that. I haven't asked.

Lock says shifter retribution is swift and proportionate, and that's good enough for me.

When Vince returned to the territory, I could see he'd found peace at last. That he'd gotten justice for his family.

"I think Aiden is old enough now to go out into the world by himself," Lock says.

"Ellie will be supervising, of course."

He reaches for my hand across the table. "It'll be great to spend some time just the two of us."

"So happens I've got some plans for you tonight, as soon as Aiden's gone down," I say.

I hear his breath catch. "What kind of plans?"

"Naked ones."

Heat flares in those intense eyes of his, and a thrill goes through me. We mated *a lot* while I was pregnant. He couldn't get enough of my pregnant belly swelling with his young, and we had sex at least twice a day right up until Aiden was born. Since then, we've had to be a little more gentle, but I'm dying to get back to our wild, take-me-anywhere mating.

I SLIP through our bedroom door and close it softly behind me. "Deeply asleep," I say. "Baby monitor on—"

I don't get to finish the sentence because Lock is on me. He pulls me onto his lap, pressing burning kisses to my neck and chest. Burying his face in my cleavage, he makes short work of the buttons on the front of my dress, then my nursing bra.

I'm self-conscious about my post-baby body, but he worships every inch of it with his tongue, drawing my big nipples into his mouth and sucking gently. When he flips me onto my back and presses his face to my panties, I try to push him away.

"Lock, this was supposed to be about you," I protest.

"This is about me," he growls, stripping my panties off in a second

The next thing I know, my thighs are wide apart and his face is buried in my pussy.

Oh god, his tongue is the best. I lie back and give myself over to it. To the appreciative sounds he's making as he laps me eagerly. To the way he works me up so skillfully. When he latches onto my clit, I start to tremble all over. I clap my hand over my mouth. It's not easy keeping quiet while my gorgeous mate drives me wild.

"Lock," I'm going to—" I whisper, a moment before I explode right in his face. He keeps right on, licking up my juices.

When he stands up, I see how much he's been enjoying himself. His cock has tented out the front of his pants. He never wears underwear, so when I unfasten the zipper, it springs out, huge and swollen, precum leaking from the head. Before he can shove it in my aching pussy, I open my mouth and take him in.

"Oh, Zoe, baby," he mutters, his hands sliding into my hair.

I love sucking his cock. Love how trembly those big muscular legs of his get. Love the way he tries not to thrust into my mouth, but winds up doing it anyway. I love the sounds he makes, the way he whispers my name over and over.

I look up at him as I try to take him in deep, keeping my eyes locked onto his.

"Oh, god," he mutters, his hips making little jerks as his cock hits the back of my throat. Then he pulls out. "Gotta be inside you, baby."

He flips me over on the bed again, raises my ass just where he wants it and enters me from behind.

I stifle a cry as his huge cock sinks into me. So big, so much to take, but I'm dripping wet. He pushes in to the hilt, his hips butting up against my ass. Then he holds me tight while he thrusts, working my clit, making me come again and again around his thick shaft.

And he doesn't quit until I'm weak and breathless. Satisfied, like always, by my sexy bear mate.

THE END

READ THE OTHER BOOKS IN THE SERIES

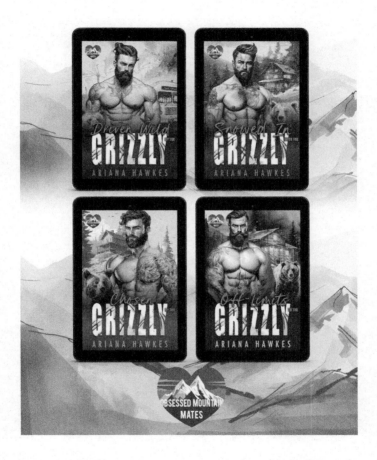

If you like fated-mate romances, with plenty of V-card fun and tons of feels, check out the other books in the series at:

arianahawkes.com/obsessed-mountain-mates

READ MY OTHER OBSESSED MATES SERIES

If you like steamy insta-love romance, featuring obsessed, growly heroes who'll do anything for their mates, check out my Obsessed Mates series. All books are standalone and can be read in any order.

Get started at arianahawkes.com/obsessed-mates

READ THE REST OF MY CATALOGUE

MateMatch Outcasts: a matchmaking agency for beasts, and the women tough enough to love them.

★★★★★ "A super **exciting, funny, thrilling, suspenseful and steamy shifter romance series**. The characters jump right off the page!"

★★★★★ "**Absolutely Freaking Fantastic**. I loved every single word of this story. It is so full of **exciting twists that will keep you guessing until the very end** of this book. I can't wait to see what might happen next in this series."

Ragtown is a small former ghost town in the mountains, populated by outcast shifters. It's a secretive place, closed-off to the outside world - until someone sets up a secret mail-order bride service that introduces women looking for their mates.

Get started at arianahawkes.com/matematch-outcasts

MY OTHER MATCHMAKING SERIES

My bestselling *Shiftr: Swipe Left For Love* series features Shiftr, the secret dating app that brings curvy girls and sexy shifters their perfect match! Fifteen books of totally bingeworthy reading — and my readers tell me that Shiftr is their favorite app ever! ;-) Get started at arianahawkes. com/shiftr

★★★★★ "**Shiftr is one of my all-time favorite series!** The stories are funny, sweet, exciting, and scorching hot! And they will **keep you glued to the pages!**"

★★★★★ "**I wish I had access to this app!** Come on, someone download it for me!"

Get started at arianahawkes.com/shiftr

CONNECT WITH ME

If you'd like to be notified about new releases, giveaways and special promotions, you can sign up to my mailing list at arianahawkes.com/mailinglist. You can also follow me on BookBub and Amazon at:

    bookbub.com/authors/ariana-hawkes

    amazon.com/author/arianahawkes

Thanks again for reading – and for all your support!

Yours,

    Ariana

* * *

USA Today bestselling author Ariana Hawkes writes spicy romantic stories with lovable characters, plenty of suspense, and a whole lot of laughs. She told her first story at the age of four, and has been writing ever since, for both work and pleasure. She lives in Massachusetts with her husband and two huskies.

www.arianahawkes.com

GET TWO FREE BOOKS

Join my mailing list and get two free books.

Once Bitten Twice Smitten

A 4.5-star rated, comedy romance featuring one kickass roller derby chick, two scorching-hot Alphas, and the naughty nip that changed their lives forever.

Lost To The Bear

He can't remember who he is. Until he meets the woman he'll never forget.

Get your free books at arianahawkes.com/freebook

READING GUIDE TO ALL OF MY BOOKS

Obsessed Mates

Her River God Wolf

Her Biker Wolf

Her Alpha Neighbor Wolf

Her Bad Boy Trucker Wolf

Her Second Chance Wolf

Her Convict Wolf

Obsessed Mountain Mates

Driven Wild By The Grizzly

Snowed In With The Grizzly

Chosen By The Grizzly

Taken Home By The Grizzly

Shifter Dating App Romances

Shiftr: Swipe Left for Love 1: Lauren

Shiftr: Swipe Left for Love 2: Dina

Shiftr: Swipe Left for Love 3: Kristin

Shiftr: Swipe Left for Love 4: Melissa

Shiftr: Swipe Left for Love 5: Andrea

Shiftr: Swipe Left for Love 6: Lori

Shiftr: Swipe Left for Love 7: Adaira

Shiftr: Swipe Left for Love 8: Timo

Shifter Holiday Romances

Bear My Holiday Hero

Ultimate Bear Christmas Magic Boxed Set Vol. 1

Ultimate Bear Christmas Magic Boxed Set Vol. 2

Printed in Great Britain
by Amazon